ALSO BY STEPHANIE MIRRO

THE LAST PHOENIX
Wings of Fire
Wings of Winter
Wings of Magic
Wings of Life
Wings of Deceit
Wings of Mercy

IMMORTAL RELICS
Curse of the Vampire
Fury of the Gods
Revenge of the Witch
Rise of the Demons

COLLECTIONS
The Outsiders: An Hourlings Anthology

WINGS OF DEATH

OF

THE LAST PHOENIX: BOOK TWO

STEPHANIE MIRRO

TANNHAUSER PRESS

Dedication

For any dreamers who think they aren't good enough. You are.

CHAPTER 1

Thursday Morning

Today was the day. With any luck, the judge would sentence Xavier to beheading, and I could finally stop fantasizing about said beheading. Brutal? Maybe, but the Master Vampire had tried to add me to his collection of exotic pretty things by way of soul theft and murder. He wasn't exactly redeemable, which made death the only viable option for a guy like him.

"Hey, V," said Joe, one of my favorite regulars, breaking through my train of thought, "can you make a little bird in the foam?"

I glanced up from behind the espresso machine where I had just started pulling his shots. From his perch on the bar stool, he gave me a wink before reaching a hand up to ensure each strand of his thick black hair was slicked back in its proper place. His sleek grey business suit, precisely tailored to fit his slender frame, and those Italian loafers were as much a constant as his hair style, even if he did need hair dye to achieve the look.

I grinned. "Anything for you, Joe."

Today was going to be a good day.

Only a week had passed, but it no longer bothered me that the supernatural Community knew that I, Veronica Neill, and my alter ego the Falcon were one and the same. Especially people I considered close enough to be friends like Joe.

The Morning Grind coffee shop where I worked my day job wasn't terribly busy that Thursday at mid-morning, which meant no one was close enough to hear our conversation at the main bar top. Most of the local crowd had come and gone. The grinders, steamers, and overall loudness of the various machines would have helped mask the words if we were busier, but only two other metal and wood stools stood along the bar, and both were empty at the moment anyway. Set along the open brick side wall, the four rustic industrial-style tables in the shop were far enough away it wouldn't have mattered if we spoke normally.

I'd been working here for about three years, ever since I quit my corporate job. Until this past week, what I used to do at night wasn't *technically* legal by our Community standards—and no, I don't mean hooking. I had started acquiring supernatural goods that fell into human hands. Okay, yeah, I was a thief and usually a damn good one, until this last botched job. In all fairness to myself, I was set up.

But after the whole Xavier incident outed my alter ego,

I switched to acquiring goods in a more legal fashion. The new jobs didn't have the same sense of danger and adventure, but they meant less chance of death.

So there was that.

You would think relieving humans of magical goods before they hurt themselves or something would be a praise-worthy job, but the angels still saw it as breaking and entering and theft. Making my case more difficult to argue was the fact that some of my customers weren't super high on the morality scale. Like Xavier, for example. Talk about a big fucking oops.

"Carmella wanted me to tell you thank you," Joe said, his voice dropping close to a whisper. "Duke Ó Faoláin didn't deserve to go that way."

When the milk finished steaming, I removed the pitcher for Joe's latte from the machine and cleaned off the steaming wand. A rich cafecito was much more common in Miami, with the strong Cuban influence here; but Joe, born Giovanni, was an Italian through and through. Well, other than actually being one of the fae like the late duke, Broderick Ó Faoláin. His ability to glamour away his distinctive fae features allowed him to move about the human world without outing the Community.

"No one deserves what happened to him," I said sadly, remembering the crime scene photos of the duke's murder that had nearly made me vomit into a trash can.

Removing a fae's wings was blasphemy, and that evil act had been done *before* Sophia, the rogue grim reaper working with Xavier, stole Broderick's soul and ended his life. A slight shudder rocked my shoulders. The Master Vampire of Miami might not have planned to steal my soul, but he had plenty of other ways to torture me for the next few hundred years.

I removed the ceramic mug now filled with rich espresso from beneath the machine and slowly poured steamed milk on top, moving my hand in such a way to create a bird in the foam, its wings spread in flight. Before handing it over, I took a quick snapshot on my phone. Social media went wild for well-done coffee art, and I could be such a sucker for praise sometimes.

"The queen has used this whole ordeal as another reason to call our kind back." Joe shook his head, his upper lip curling in disgust as he raised the mug to his mouth. "That she would use the duke's death to push her own political agenda just proves how self-righteous she truly is."

I didn't have much to say to that. The last week had taught me more about fae politics than I had known my entire life…which wasn't saying much since my knowledge was close to zero before all this. I was nowhere near an expert or even proficient at the subject, but at least I could fake it a little better these days.

The fae queen had made it clear she wanted all her kind to return to the Otherworld, a magical realm that existed parallel to this one. Most of the Community presumed it was because she wasn't a fan of half-bloods. The word for them in their native language meant more along the lines of bastard, but I could never remember what it was. Studying wasn't really my priority growing up, either. Dyslexia will do that to a kid.

Regardless, they were the nine-months-later result of a fae and a human—or any other species—deciding to have a baby or, more often, just getting down and dirty between the sheets without protection. She hadn't said anything to stop that presumption from growing, either. Fae weren't exactly known in the Community for their humble personalities, and half-blood orphans were only becoming more common.

Joe wasn't a half-blood, but he had been born in the human realm, grew up in Italy, and considered it his home. As one of the few people I actually got to know past acquaintance status in recent times, I liked having him around, and the idea of not being able to see him again weighed heavy on my heart. Not many fae were as kind and friendly as him, even others descended from the Summer Court like he was.

"I hope the opposition is able to show her the error of her ways," I said at last, steaming milk for the next order.

"Ah, I am boring you, sì?" he laughed.

"You never bore me, Joe," I said with a quick smile. "I'm just distracted about…this afternoon."

He nodded, a knowing gleam in his eye. "He'll get what he deserves."

My boss Isaac huffed up on my left, out of breath as usual. Thinning grey hair barely covered his glistening head, but bushy eyebrows of the same hue more than made up for the hair loss. His portly belly made the apron he wore stick out away from his clothes, which meant he always left his shifts with some sort of stain on his uncovered khaki shorts. He'd gained a bunch of weight after his wife left him a few years ago. I almost felt bad for him except he wasn't my favorite person, nor was I his. A mutual dislike.

"Veronica, I need you to work a few extra hours today," he said, wiping a bead of sweat off his forehead with a napkin. "Chloe called out, and I've got to get this supply order finished."

Joe waved goodbye as he finished his latte and slid off the stool. I kissed the air twice as if kissing both his cheeks before turning back to Isaac.

"I can't today," I said, honestly feeling bad. I hated leaving my coworkers with less than a full crew. I slid a fresh pitcher of milk under the steaming wand and started it up. "I've got an appointment."

"Can't you reschedule it?" Isaac's tone made it clear he didn't believe my answer, which wasn't new.

"No."

He clucked his tongue. "I'm really disappointed in your lack of effort lately."

Rising anger made my hand shake as I removed the steamed milk from the machine and cleaned off the wand. Wiping that disapproving look off his face with the real reason I couldn't stay would be so satisfying. I couldn't exactly ask the Death Enforcement Agency—you know, the one governed by angels—to reschedule the sentencing of a Master Vampire. But sharing that fact with a human who had no idea the supernatural world existed would only land me back into trouble, and I'd had enough of that for one lifetime.

Also, there was no way I would miss a chance to see Thane Munro again. He had some questions to answer, like why he was avoiding me. Not only was I looking forward to seeing if the agent's touch still caused some inexplicable, unladylike reactions in my body, but he had promised to find out more about my brother's murder.

"It's not exactly fair to fault me for making an appointment outside of my scheduled hours." I kept my expression as neutral as possible while I poured the milk into a mug to finish a cafe con leche.

Isaac let out a huff of indignation. "This is hardly the first time. You've been slacking."

"Slacking?" I couldn't stop my glare as I practically slammed the nearly empty pitcher down on the counter. The remaining milk splashed over the side. So much for staying neutral, but the last week and a half was rough. I'd almost died more than once and almost had to out myself as a phoenix to the entire DEA and a nest of vampires. And not just any phoenix—the *last* phoenix. "I had one bad day because I came down with the flu, and you call that slacking?"

Sure, my best friend Kit had forged the doctor's note, but Isaac didn't know that. My blood was starting to boil, and it didn't help my current situation that my kind already ran pretty hot.

He smiled at a customer who turned to look at the commotion. Lowering his voice, he said, "Do not embarrass me in front of our customers and your coworkers."

"You don't need *my* help to embarrass you," I said, though I did keep myself from yelling like I wanted to. I finished the drink and called out the order.

"You are on thin ice," Isaac hissed through his teeth. "If you keep this up, I'll—"

"What?" I interrupted, putting my hands on my hips and staring him down. "Fire me?"

He spluttered as he tried to come up with something to say back. The man was used to bossing around high school and college kids at their first jobs, kids who typically backed down, though often with a resulting sulk.

"Save your breath. You might give yourself a heart attack." I practically ripped off my apron and threw it on the counter, wincing slightly as my ribs groaned in protest, still not quite healed from my fight with the vampires. "My shift is over anyway. Let me know when I'm welcome back for my next one."

After grabbing my purse from the cubby beneath the counter, I waved to my coworkers and left. The heat and wetness in the air outside greeted me like an old friend, immediately bringing my anger down a notch.

Most of the people I knew in Miami were accustomed to the oppressive humidity and constant ring of sweat around their armpits, but that didn't mean they didn't like to complain about it any chance they got. I might have been alone in my love for the heat, to the point that I only drank my coffee hot all year long, but the warmth also felt really good on my sore bones today.

I had taken a beating—almost been eaten alive if I wanted to get technical—and an angel's healing had only put the bones back together and closed up the cuts and bites. Time would have to heal the rest.

I sighed as I waited for a city bus to pass before crossing the street. I didn't know why I kept the barista job after everything that happened last week. The Community knew who I was, and I didn't need a day job as a cover anymore. My work acquiring goods gave me more money than I could have ever hoped for in my previous corporate career. I loved coffee, but that didn't mean I needed to make it for anyone but me.

Maybe I could become a professional latte artist, attend competitions and all that. Yeah, that sounded much nicer than dealing with Isaac's bullshit.

Heading for an alley just another block down and squeezed between a restaurant and a thrift shop, I checked my watch. It was late morning, which meant I had just over an hour to shower and get over to DEA headquarters before the sentencing started.

I clenched my teeth, hoping the hour would give me enough time to cool down from the argument with my boss as well. The last thing I needed was to go into the courtroom already riled up and ready for a fight.

After a quick glance up and down the strip mall's sidewalk to make sure anyone around was preoccupied with their own lives, I turned into the alley. I hadn't driven that morning, but I wanted to get ready at my secret penthouse apartment rather than my smaller one close to the coffee shop. I had stayed close by over the last week so my pseudo guardian angel, Jessa, could check in on me.

The luxurious atmosphere at the Brickell Flatiron would help soothe my worries and keep the throb building in my temple from getting any worse—stress could be such a dick—but I also kept the place hidden from everyone except my best friend Kit. Even from Jessa.

As the angel assigned to keep me alive after my brother's death, Jessa didn't watch me 24/7, she just kept an ear out for anything or anyone that might cause me harm. The whole mess with Xavier wasn't her fault; her boss let me take the fall to find the real soul stealer among his own ranks.

Just past the two side doors of the adjoining shops, the narrow alley ended at a dumpster and a wall. I was just about to shift into my other form when I got there, but something hard pressed into the middle of my back.

"Hand over your purse," said a gruff voice.

I groaned out loud. "You have *got* to be kidding me."

"Hurry up." The assumed gun pushed harder into my back. My bruised ribs cried out in protest.

"Listen, guy," I held up my hands, though I had no intention of complying with his demand. "I've had a really rough week, and I'm not a good target. Walk away and go find someone else to rob."

"I didn't ask for your opinion, bitch." A click indicated he pulled back the hammer.

I did warn him.

Before he could pull the trigger, I whipped around and disarmed him. Pointing the gun back in his face, I smirked. The man turned out to be a kid who probably wasn't even old enough to buy liquor. He gaped at me beneath his dark hooded sweatshirt, beads of sweat dripping down his face. Miami was way too fucking hot for that outfit.

"I'm going to keep this gun as a memento of our short time together, okay?" I used the gun to shoo him away, and his sneakers beat a fast tempo on the cement as he listened this time.

That was the most action I'd seen in a week, and most definitely not the type of action I needed. I cleared the round, removed the magazine, and tossed those and the gun into the dumpster. Muttering to myself, I shifted into my falcon form and flapped my wings to gain height.

I glanced back as movement caught my eye, which turned out to be the ultraviolet light of someone kneeling next to the dumpster at the end of an alley. The wide eyes of a homeless man stared up at me as I caught the wind current and winged away.

Shit.

Today was not going well at all.

CHAPTER 2

Thursday Afternoon

When I arrived downtown at the Death Enforcement Agency courtroom an hour later, the place was packed, every row of seating filled. I guess I wasn't the only one who wanted to see the motherfucker burn. Or watch his head roll. Whatever the judge decided was fine by me as long as it included him turning to dust and bones.

Technically, today was just the sentencing, but it was one step closer to justice. Xavier Garcia had hurt a lot of people, and he was found guilty of his crimes—murder, torture, assault, and kidnapping, just to name a few. I had almost been next, a fact that always made my hands sweat as they did now. I wiped my palms as discreetly as possible on my dark jeans while searching for an empty seat.

The courtroom was large enough to hold five hundred or so people on rows of pew-style wooden benches in the gallery. A desk for the judge sat on a raised platform at the very back of the room, facing those gathered. Even though the court was governed by the DEA and the angelic choir, the Florida state flag hung on one side of the wall behind the judge's desk and the Community flag on the other.

As the Master Vampire of Miami, Xavier's job had been to keep his creations in line, work with the local hospitals to keep his people fed and happy, and otherwise keep the human and Community populations of Miami alone. He failed to do any of that properly. Some tried to blame his actions on a vampire's general bloodlust, rising from the grave sans soul, or centuries of oppression—an argument that had me snorting in derision since vampires were among the wealthiest people on the planet—but none of the other Master Vampires ever attempted what Xavier had, which quickly negated that argument.

I scanned the rows of people, noting those who sat hunched over, those with bruised faces and bandaged arms. His victims. My lungs constricted, my breaths becoming shallow as I saw them for the first time, knowing how close I had come to being among their ranks. Those unfortunate souls who were caught and tortured by Xavier.

But also those fortunate enough to have made it out alive. Others had not been so lucky.

Their eyes darted around the room, and they jumped at the smallest sounds. Most of their physical injuries were healed, but how long would it take to heal the emotional wounds?

My best friend Kit caught my eye from where she sat a few benches up and waved me over. I took a deep breath and held my head high as I walked down the middle aisle. Since I had pulled my long white-blonde hair up into a sleek ponytail, my violet irises would be visible to anyone who looked at my face. I wouldn't hide who I was anymore. Well, part of who I was. I still didn't plan to tell anyone else who or what I really was. I liked danger, but not that much danger.

The whispers started immediately. People didn't know what to do around me. I had brought down a Master Vampire, with a little help of course. No small feat and thoroughly awe-inspiring. Or maybe terror-inducing was a better fit, even if I had almost died. Whatever the word, I also lived the last few years as a thief, and some still considered me capable of murder despite the DEA clearing my name.

Can't win them all, I suppose.

When I reached Kit's pew, the Community members who had to stand to let me pass didn't seem to mind my presence, at least. I even heard a murmured thank you, but when I turned to respond, no one would make eye contact with me. After a quick nod to acknowledge whomever spoke, I continued toward Kit.

I adjusted my black blazer as I sat, letting out a small squeak of discomfort as I jostled my ribs, then leaned toward Kit and whispered, "A packed house to watch a man die, huh? Does that make us all sadists?"

She threw me a look, her dark brown eyes full of disdain.

I held up my hands in a sign of surrender. "Kidding. No need to put a hex on me."

"I didn't think you'd make it on time," she said, brushing her braids back behind a shoulder as she turned to watch the front again. The shaved side of her head faced me, the buzzed hair getting a bit too long to make out the pattern. She'd create a new one soon, usually a book reference or some kind of sci-fi symbol.

"Surprising, right?" I was late to one event and she never let me live it down. Embracing her taunt was the only option at this point.

Kit was an enigma to most people. With both Cuban and Dominican genetics, her skin was that beautiful shade of brown that appeared when an espresso shot finished pulling, almost caramel-like, and smooth as marble. The girl never broke out—ever. But what did she choose to do with that perfect skin? She decorated it with tattoos galore. One whole sculpted arm was sleeved, and she was fast at work on the other. I wouldn't be surprised if models wept in horror after she passed by.

I liked tattoos, just not on myself. I preferred a golden, coffee-with-creamer hue, sans tan lines, which I could maintain lounging on my penthouse terrace in the buff almost all year long.

I digress. The point is, most people would not peg Kit as a technological mastermind capable of hacking into the DEA's security system, especially considering her outfit of the day for a courtroom included ripped jeans and a t-shirt that read "What the FRAK?" Whatever the fuck that meant.

But most people would be wrong. She was a goddamn genius.

"New bling?" I asked, nodding to her nose ring after she raised an eyebrow at me.

She tapped the green stone in the middle of the silver hoop. "Malachite. Its properties should help keep my negative energy at bay."

Kit was also a witch, though she had given up practicing most magic and devoted her life to tech after World War II. It was a long, depressing story involving a genocide she helped carry out, and it was her own to tell someday. So, let's just say she wasn't super happy with those who governed the witches and warlocks and pretty much renounced their way of life.

Their loss, my gain.

"Did you bring any extra malachite for me?" I asked.

"No."

"Will it work on me if I snuggle you?"

"No."

"What about if I just hold your hand?"

"No."

I opened my mouth to heckle her some more, but the door to the left of the judge's desk opened and the whole room fell silent.

It was time.

Two guards escorted Xavier into the courtroom, thick iron chains clanking around his hands and feet, his gait halting as the manacles limited his stride. Above the bright orange hue of his prison uniform, red highlights in his otherwise rich brown hair seemed even brighter. The strands reached his chin and looked like they were washed and brushed that day, except that was just one of the perks of being an ancient immortal creature—no need to wash his hair. It stayed luscious all on its own.

When he raised his dark gaze to meet mine, my heart leaped to my throat, blocking my airway and urging my flight response to get me the fuck out of there. And then he smirked. The goddamn bloodsucker had the balls to smirk at me. Clenching my fists at my sides to keep from launching myself at him, my fear turned to simmering anger about to boil over. I could not wait for him to die, only I wished I could be the one to do it.

The attendees and I stood as one when a guard asked us to, a nervous energy binding us together in a mutual hatred of this vampire. The judge came in next, his iridescent white wings tucked behind his back as he strode to his seat and waved us all to sit again.

Unlike a human court and justice system, the Community had no need of lawyers—the angels were the end-all-be-all. Their word was justice in this human realm, regardless of the fact that humans and the Community alike all worshipped different gods and goddesses, who did, in fact, exist. Millennia ago, part of the agreement to initially allow other supernatural types into the human realm required us to be completely obedient to the angels' laws.

The judge was one such archangel whose word was law, and an old one if his shimmering white hair was any indication. I actually didn't know, but he looked older than Adam, the grim reapers' boss, so I made an assumption. I was probably wrong.

After we sat, I kind of blacked out—not literally, but I honestly couldn't remember what anyone said if I tried. My hatred for the vampire who wanted to own and breed me like a broodmare filled every fiber of my being and manifested as trembling in every part of my body. It took all my energy and a death grip on the bench's seat to stay where I was and keep my shaking from becoming noticeable. I had tunnel vision as I stared at the side of Xavier's face, willing my rage to murder him where he sat.

Alas, I didn't have that kind of power. He knew the truth of who I was, but he chose to keep that knowledge to himself.

But for how much longer?

I only came to after Kit nudged me. I glanced at her, startled, and she tilted her head to the side, back behind me. When I turned to look, the rage all but vanished, replaced by something close to rapturous desire.

Thane Munro.

Why in Dazhbog's name did this grim reaper affect me so strongly, even after a week of not seeing him? He was a dead guy for fuck's sake. I could do better. Sure, he was quite possibly the hottest man to ever walk the earth, with his velvety black hair, swoon-worthy deep ocean-blue eyes, and lightly tanned skin that reminded me of the creamy, delicious first sip of a freshly made latte. I caught myself just before I licked my lips.

But his looks didn't mean he was good in bed or a decent partner in life. Quite the opposite was more likely. Men who were too pretty usually didn't have to try too hard, and for some unknown reason, most women let them get away with it. I wondered if I would let him get away with a sub-par experience for a chance to see his—

Sun above, I sounded like a horny high schooler again.

The reaper turned his head toward me, catching my gaze and giving me a wink as if he heard my thoughts. A flutter tickled my stomach. I rolled my eyes at him and turned my attention back to the front only to find Xavier had turned to stare at me intently with narrowed eyes. He glanced at Thane, then back at me.

Well, well, well. Seemed like Mr. Master Vampire didn't like his so-called things touched by anyone else. If only there was time to have some fun with that. My lips twisted into a smirk before he turned around.

"Xavier Garcia, you have been found guilty of crimes against humanity and the Community," the judge said in his concluding speech. "To pay for these crimes, I sentence you to death by beheading. The sentencing will be carried out just before dusk this coming Monday. Court is adjourned."

He banged his gavel and stood, leaving the same way he came in. As soon as his door shut, the courtroom erupted in cheers and applause, some even booing Xavier while the guards led him away. The delay in carrying out his death was typical, though still irritating—even the agency had paperwork to fill out and process. The Master Vampire cast one last glance back at me, catching my eye between the shoulders and heads in front of me. He had the audacity to wink.

Despite knowing that he was going to die—for real— in just a few short days, dread settled around my shoulders and goosebumps rose along my arms. Only he would be so narcissistic to wink at someone he tried to enslave, moments after being sentenced to death by decapitation.

So why did his nonchalance unsettle me so much?

After following everyone else out of the courtroom and

into the headquarters' foyer—both rooms sharing the first floor to keep prying eyes out of the reapers' business—I parted ways with Kit. She had business to attend to, and I planned to catch Thane and ask him about my brother's file.

Only he caught me first.

Warmth crept up behind me. I turned to look at the cause, and there he was. He had his hands tucked into his navy-blue dress slacks, and his white button-down top was left open enough to display a hint of hardened pecs. His familiar smirk pulled at his lips, those luscious, full lips I craved to feel all over my body. I wanted to swoon into his arms, except I was most definitely not a swooning kind of girl.

Maybe I could be persuaded to be one if the right guy came along. Roleplaying was supposed to be fun, right?

"Nice to see you on your feet again," Thane said, a twinkle of mischief in his eyes, "without vomiting."

Ugh, he just had to remind me that the last time I saw him I threw up at his feet. Angelic healing aftereffects at their finest.

"Yeah, well, you've been avoiding me," I said, crossing my arms.

He ran a hand through his mop of dark hair. "Not intentionally. Things have been… chaotic."

"You owe me."

"I know, and I will deliver."

"When?"

"How does tomorrow sound?" he asked.

"If that's the best you can do." I didn't bother to hide the annoyance in my tone. He'd had over a week already.

He sighed. "Listen, a lot has been going on around here,

not just with this case."

My eyebrows pulled together, curiosity instantly engaged. "Like what?"

"I'm not permitted to discuss it." His gaze darted around the foyer, which had mostly emptied of Community members there for the sentencing. Only a few stragglers like us remained, chatting in small groups of twos and threes.

I let out a huff. "Then why bring it up?"

His eyes met mine, the dark blue shade lightening to sapphire. "I wanted you to know I wasn't avoiding you on purpose."

If I didn't get out of there soon, I was going to kiss him. "Noted. Call me when you have the file ready."

I turned, my ponytail flaring out behind me, and headed for the door. It's not that I wanted to be mean or even play coy, but that man did something to me that no other ever had. I was drawn to him in an inexplicable way, as if his scorching touch would ignite something within me. Something new. Possibly dangerous.

I just didn't know if I was ready to find out what that was yet.

CHAPTER 3

Thursday Afternoon

My feelings for Thane obviously hadn't changed, especially now that I knew he wasn't avoiding me, just busy. My heart did a little pitter-patter at the onslaught of images of how he could make it up to me. I pushed open the door leading out of DEA headquarters and collided with someone about to come in.

"Oh!" I stumbled backward a step, hitting the doorframe and grunting from my bumped bruises. A hand reached out to steady me.

"My apologies, my mind must have been elsewhere," said a man's voice.

Wincing, I glanced up, ready to give this man a piece of

my mind for not watching where he was going—ignoring the fact that I, too, had my thoughts elsewhere, because now I was in pain—but my breath caught in my throat.

He was a fae, and a fairly attractive one at that. They all were, thanks to their naturally immortal genetics, but I hadn't seen one this up close and personal before. Well, other than Joe, who did his best to hide his fae features. The sun peeked out from behind a cloud right then, its warm rays falling on the man like magic. His light brown hair glittered with previously hidden streaks of red, rendering it a shade of auburn that reminded me of fall in the Appalachian Mountains. I had only been once, but the memory would remain forever.

Friendly blue-green eyes shifted from one color to the other as they met mine. Friendly and fae were not usually two words that went together like peanut butter and jelly, but they suited this man and his smile very well. His skin was the color of freshly poured milk, only it had the slightest hint of gold running through the veins like caramel.

Like all fae out and about on human streets, he had glamoured himself to hide his inhuman features from anyone outside the Community. His dark blue jeans and untucked mint-green polo helped him blend in even more. He was of slimmer stature than Thane, more palm tree than oak, but his muscles were just as well-defined as the reaper's.

I shook my head, realizing I was staring. "No apologies necessary. I also had my thoughts on something else." Or some*one*.

He held out a hand. "I'm Colin Ó Broin."

"Veronica Neill," I said as I gripped his.

When he brought my hand to his lips, his eyebrows rose

slightly. Unlike Joe from the coffee shop, who was also one of the seelie fae—the only kind allowed in the human realm—the power emanating through this fae's touch set all the hairs on my body standing on end. His lighter eye color indicated he belonged to the Spring Court, known for their wildly fluctuating magical abilities. Some were hardly more than humans with no innate talents, and some were close to gods. This one here was a being who could kill a person with very little effort.

His eyes never left mine, and a slight tingle of excitement swept through me, suppressing the fear. This guy may have been a fae and not my typical go-to for dating, but he was also alive. Not something I used to consider in the past, but he had something Thane sure as hell didn't.

"It's a pleasure to meet the mighty hero," he said, releasing me. A strange sense of disappointment left my hand feeling empty.

We stepped to the side to allow someone to pass through the door, back into the foyer I just left. The DEA headquarters shared an expansive courtyard with several other high-rise office buildings. Wooden benches and palm trees surrounded a fountain that was home to many hopeful wishes, if the glittering at the bottom was any indication.

I smiled a bit sheepishly when the door closed again. "I wouldn't go as far as calling me a hero. Let's just say a head was on the line, and that head was mine."

"And so humble." He grinned.

I laughed. "That's not something I've been accused of before."

"Just falsely accused of murder and theft," he said, his eyes twinkling.

"Of *that* theft, at any rate." I winked to make my point. His laugh reminded me of my father's, robust and full of mirth. It made me smile.

"I, unfortunately, have business to attend to inside, but it would be my absolute pleasure to get to know you better." His eyes shifted to a lighter teal when he smiled. "If it's not too forward of me to ask, may I take you to dinner someday soon?"

I'd be lying if I said my heart didn't do another little pitter-patter. Someone was actually asking me out on a date—and I liked it. "Forward can be good."

We swapped numbers, and I had to bite my lip to keep my excitement from showing. Couldn't come across too desperate or he might change his mind.

"Until we meet again," he said, lifting a hand in farewell.

I smiled again as he headed inside the building. After turning toward the busy Miami streets, I practically skipped away.

Reaper who?

The morning after the sentencing, I had a completely legal meeting with a new client in *el Mercado Sombra*, the Shadow Market. The hidden-from-human-eyes location was a sanctuary for people like me because whatever entity or power had created the street and shops inside forbade anyone from using magic within its confines.

El Mercado was one of my favorite places since being outed to the Community. I no longer had to worry about keeping my identity safe, and people were actually friendly to me. Not that they weren't nice before, but I was more reclusive in the past and usually ignored any attempts at conversation. Maybe I could even start making some new friends for the first time in… Well, I never really made Community friends besides Kit.

I left my penthouse by way of the wind, shifting into my bird form just before launching myself off the balcony. That first moment of free fall was always exhilarating, before I caught the breeze beneath my wings and glided. I swung out over the ocean first, diving low to feel the salty sea spray coating the fire-colored feathers normally hidden beneath the outer browns and greys when my wings were tucked in. Sailboats, yachts, and cruise ships spread across the ocean as far as the eye could see, but the only sounds were the cresting waves and an occasional seagull. Heaven.

One of the huge perks to being a shapeshifter was not worrying about how to bring my clothes, purse, and weapons along with me—anything I had on me stayed exactly where it was while my human form moved to a completely static parallel dimension and the bird form came out to play. Wounds were the only thing that transferred from one form to the other. Such a bummer.

Growing up, our parents forbade Maddox and me from becoming too comfortable around humans, and they also kept our existence a secret from most of the Community— so much so that everyone in the Community believed the phoenix kind to be extinct. Those few members who knew our parents only knew them as shapeshifters, though they refrained from disclosing what type of shifter, and it was considered poor etiquette to ask. Unless you were a reaper or angel, of course.

After my parents returned to the sun and I rose from

their ashes, I began to venture into the supernatural world, but I was very careful to keep Mad out of it. At least I thought I was careful.

It wasn't that I faulted my parents for their fears—we were the last of our kind, the last phoenixes. With their final deaths and then Mad's before he gained his rebirth ability, it was just me left. They did what they thought necessary to keep our species alive, allowing me to manifest all of my fiery rebirth abilities through their return to the sun. A lonely thought in the beginning, and worse without Mad's laughter ringing in my ears, but hopefully I could start to change that.

I would need to if I wanted my kind to continue.

After getting my fill of the ocean breezes and even a quick snack—eating raw fish straight from the source wasn't as gross a thought to a bird of prey—I flapped my wings and headed back toward the mainland. With avian vision, ultraviolet lights allowed me to see the world in hues otherwise invisible to the human eye. The city was bright during the day, shades of pinks and purples, blues and greens that mixed together in a cacophony of color.

The market had a variety of entrances, but I favored one in particular due to the gatekeeper: the piano shop. I still used it even though the owner and one of my favorite people in the world, Tony, had taken a much-needed vacation after his encounter with Xavier left him on death's doorstep. But not with any physical scars, thankfully. Community healers could be almost as efficient as angels.

After alighting in an alley close by and shifting back into human form—a delightfully instantaneous experience—I entered Tony's piano store. I didn't know the younger gentleman who watched the shop for my friend, and he didn't strike me as the chatty type since his nose remained stuck behind a book despite the bell ringing above the door, so I didn't linger before heading straight for the velvet curtain at the back. When it whispered my name, the magic of the market pulled the veil back and allowed me inside.

I took my time strolling down the winding paved street that wouldn't have existed to a human, or at least not to one without a pass. To any other human, only a storage room existed behind the curtain.

The heat grew thicker inside the market as the breeze fought to gain entry around the surrounding buildings, and the sun beat down on my bare legs. Linen shorts and a loose-fitting tank top had been the right call today.

El Mercado was mostly made up of stalls set up outside, their canvas roofs curving right along with the hidden street. Only a few shops like the computer lab and The Witch's Brew were able to acquire the coveted indoor spaces, which were few and far between thanks to the market's squeezed-in-beside-reality nature. Air conditioning and shelter from storms came at a steep premium.

My meeting wasn't set to start for another fifteen minutes (take that, Kit), so I stopped at one of the brightly colored stalls where clothing racks overflowed with a variety of designs for any age. A one-stop shop under a canvas roof. I pushed aside hanger after hanger of shirts and dresses, not really intending to buy, just enjoying the simple experience without a warrant for my arrest along with a hefty reward enticing anybody to ruin the moment.

In the past, all my contracts were handled in the market's computer lab, set up with a security system no magic or hacker could penetrate. Privacy was valued highly in our world, and not even Kit's setup could mimic the lab's, despite her best efforts. She came close, though it still pissed her off whenever the topic came up. I tried to avoid it.

After the DEA cleared my name of Broderick's murder and soul theft, dozens of requests flooded my inbox. My previous contracts were always to track down and steal back magical items of great—and potentially lethal—power that fell into the wrong hands. Although, as I learned, some of my clients' hands weren't much better.

Maybe it was a bit arrogant of me, but I always assumed the angels left me alone because the objects I recovered were still more dangerous for human hands. The way I saw it, I was doing them a favor.

But now, the requests were for more mundane things like tracking down a family heirloom or locating a lost lover—I figured that guy wasn't so much lost as fled. One young man even asked me out on a date. I smiled ruefully at the memory of his email. Unfortunately for him, finding dates online wasn't really my thing. Dating in general hadn't been much of a priority in the past, but I might just reconsider that going forward.

"Things seem to be getting worse these days," a woman's voice caught my attention.

She and another lady browsed the rack of clothing across from mine. Both appeared to be closing in on middle-age if the tiny bit of white in the speaking woman's blonde roots and her friend's crow's feet were accurate indicators. Although middle-age could be anywhere from 40 to 400 years old (or more) depending on their species.

"It's no wonder their queen wants them all to return," the other woman said, shaking her head in agreement. Thick, straight brown hair fell past her shoulders. She held a shirt up to her chest before putting it back.

Their ears weren't visible, but it didn't take a genius to know these women weren't fae. The only other queen I knew of was the vampire queen, and her kind didn't usually come out shopping in broad daylight. I continued to slide through hangers, though I wasn't really focused on the clothes anymore as I eavesdropped.

The first woman, Blondie, dropped her voice and glanced around, though she didn't really strike me as someone who cared who overheard. It wasn't like she was whispering even now. "Did you hear that they found yet another one?"

Brownie gasped, a hand over her heart in true dramatic fashion. "How many bodies does that make now?"

Bodies? Do tell. I sidled closer.

"Three dead, two missing," Blondie said, earning another gasp from her friend.

Goosebumps raced down my arms as my thoughts gained traction. Why hadn't I heard about any of this? Could Xavier be involved somehow, even from behind bars?

"So sad, isn't it?" Blondie clucked her tongue, then held up a shirt to her chest in front of the standing mirror. "Anyway, Brad suggested dinner…"

The two women turned to a more mundane topic of conversation as they browsed, leaving me with too few answers for all the questions I had now. I checked my watch and decided to abandon my attempt at shopping to meet with my client. I'd be a whopping five minutes early, and then maybe I could spend some time looking into this new missing persons issue.

On fair weather days like today, which meant hot and humid but no rain in Miami, the market's picnic tables were usually filled with Community members, especially teens looking for an escape from Mom and Dad. Today lived up to those expectations. I miraculously found an empty table and waited, knowing my client would be able to spot me as easily in this crowd of teeny boppers as if I wore a giant sign that read, "Hi, I'm the Falcon."

The buzz of constant chatter mixed with the few birds who inhabited the palm trees and shrubs that lined the street meandering through the market. Sizzling meats and a variety of aromatic fruits and vegetables added their sweet, mouthwatering scents to the mostly stale air. As a sanctuary for the Community, the market could be a great place to people-watch, which was exactly what I did.

A minute after our arranged meeting time, a frazzled-looking young woman hustled up, dragging a little boy who seemed intent on digging his feet into the ground.

"I'm so sorry I'm late." She blew dark brown hair out of her face with a quick breath, and helped the boy, no older than three, sit on the other bench before sitting herself.

"You're only a minute late, but I wouldn't consider that late," I said with a smile.

"Oh, is that all? I thought for sure we'd never make it here before you gave up waiting." She laughed nervously, eyeing her child every few seconds as if he might run off if she looked away. He probably would have, too. They were clearly related, with the same wavy dark brown hair and distinct honey-colored eyes, set against somewhat pale skin considering where we lived. She had attempted to look put together, but frayed seams and old stains on her blouse and slacks made it clear she wasn't well off.

"Forgive me for being so rude." She held out her hand. "I'm Tabitha."

I shook her hand. "Veronica. Tell me what you need me to find." No sense dragging the conversation out to be nice. This woman had her hands full. The little boy kept trying to wiggle away from her, giggling like it was a game when she pulled him back.

"My husband passed away last year, and the pack took his body before I had a chance to…"

As Tabitha continued to ramble on with her story about her husband's wedding ring, my mind snatched the word "body" and ran away with my thoughts. I felt bad for the woman and her boy—single parenting was not for the faint of heart, especially in a werewolf family—but I couldn't help wondering about the bodies the other two women had discussed.

They never mentioned whether the bodies were human or not, or why these bodies in particular attracted their attention. Miami wasn't exactly known as a safe haven. Crime happened, and a lot of it. Yet these women made it seem like something was off about the deaths, or that they were connected somehow.

I wanted to know more.

I missed the sense of adventure and danger my job used to bring, and only a week passed since the last one—even if it did end with my near-death or capture. What was I going to do with myself if I was stuck tracking down items of no real importance for the next few hundred years? I didn't want to come off callous; the items meant quite a lot to the people seeking them, but so far none required any real stealth or secrecy.

My phone buzzed in my pocket. I glanced at Tabitha, who was still going on about the ring she wanted me to find while keeping her eyes on the boy, so I checked the message. It was from Thane: "Got the file. Meet at Kit's. Time?"

I nearly rolled my eyes, but I didn't want Tabitha to think it was about her. He didn't even bother to ask if it was okay to meet at Kit's place, which also meant he didn't want to be alone with me. This guy was fucking with my head in the worst way.

"3," I typed back.

Tabitha stopped her tirade about the alpha of her pack to grab her little boy from falling backward off the bench. His squeal of delight echoed through the picnic area, earning an equal number of smiles and glares from the other patrons. A perfect little wolf cub in the making. My stomach did a little flip-flop.

"I'll find the ring for you," I said as I stood. "Free of charge."

Her mouth dropped open as she snapped her head to look at me, nearly dropping her kid in the process. "I couldn't possibly—"

"It's not up for debate." Waving a goodbye to her and the boy, I turned and walked away before she could protest further.

I had become a bit like a mother to Mad after our parents left us nine years ago, though admittedly not a great one. He was only ten at the time. I hadn't embraced my responsibilities then, and I wished with all my heart that I could go back and do it all over again. Things would have been so different.

But something weird happened to my body when I saw Tabitha's boy nearly tip over. Listening to that little giggle directed at his mother for saving him… For the first time ever, at the ripe old age of twenty-seven—and after a poorly timed text from Thane—I felt the first hint of desire to have kids of my own.

Ugh.

CHAPTER 4

Friday Afternoon

As much as I hated to admit it, I wanted to see that damned reaper again, even if Kit was there cockblocking me. Not that she wanted to, of course. Thane had chosen her apartment as the rendezvous place, and I wasn't going to argue. I didn't know if he picked the location because he didn't want to be alone with me or because he wanted to share some news with Kit, too.

Whatever the reason, the mere thought of him put a pep in my step as I paced around my best friend's living room.

"Oh, maybe he's going to tell us about these mysterious bodies and wants you to look into it," I said, circling her couch again. Her living room was too small to pace properly, no bigger than my penthouse bedroom. Come to think of it, the rectangle that made up her living room, open-concept kitchen, and entryway was probably still smaller than my bedroom.

"For the love of all that's holy, stop pacing," Kit said from behind one of her computer screens. Her entire technological setup was tucked neatly into one corner of the living area, making the limited apartment space appear even smaller. "He's probably got a new tracking device stuck in his neck and doesn't want to bring attention to your penthouse."

I made a face at her even though she couldn't see it. Leave it to Kit to come up with a perfectly logical explanation.

"I saw that," she said.

"How?" Her face wasn't even visible behind the giant monitor.

"Magic."

"Liar."

"I have cameras in every corner."

I glanced up toward the corner above a window and made another face at the gadget pointed directly at me. Twenty-seven going on thirteen, that was me. I forgot she had installed a bunch of new security features after the manticore attack. Even the replaced windowpane was bullet proof.

"Cute," she said, the click-clack of her keyboard never stopping.

The air seemed to grow thinner, like life itself was being sucked out of the room. A moment later, Thane stepped out of his teleportation circle into the space between the living room and the kitchen, a folder tucked under one arm. When the portal closed behind him, he put the device in his pocket. Not even Kit's wards could stop a DEA agent from entering.

"Ladies." He tilted his head, a piece of velvety midnight-hued hair falling across his forehead. My breath hitched in my throat. Oh, how I wanted to brush that strand back into place before running my hands through the rest of it.

Meeting my gaze, his deep blue eyes roved over me, drinking in the length of my tanned legs. My cheeks flushed with excitement. Shorts had been a wise decision on my part. Or maybe a terrible one. I still didn't know.

"May I?" I held out a hand for the file. Distraction would be key in his presence.

He placed the manilla folder in my palm, his fingers brushing against mine. The scorching heat that came with his touch ignited me down to my core, making me breathless in its intensity. The overwhelming sensation stopped the moment his hand receded, but fading memories of his touch continued to pulse through my body.

Fuck. I needed to figure out what the hell was going on with this guy and his delicious heat. Just not until after I figured out who killed Mad and why, and also after I killed said person. Besides, there was no sense rushing the Thane thing if it meant the possibility of no longer feeling the heat. Call me a glutton for punishment, but I kind of liked the mystery.

"Thanks." I sat on the couch and opened the file.

The smiling face of my little brother stared up at me. His last school photo, taken when he was sixteen years old, followed by a list of his physical characteristics. My breath caught in my throat, and I raised a hand to cover my mouth before a sob escaped. I didn't display any photos of him at my place. The guilt was too strong.

He had been such a handsome boy, inheriting our father's white-blond hair like me, but our mother's green eyes. Like the other kids his age, he wore his hair long and in his face, a fact I always teased him about. "How do you even know what your boyfriend looks like?" I would ask, and he would groan at my awful attempt at humor. Someone had to be a parent and tell dad jokes, and that someone had been me.

If only I had taken it more seriously sooner.

Shaking my head to clear my thoughts, I turned the page. A bunch of black boxes covering most of the text stared back at me. A redacted file. My eyebrows pulled together as I flipped through page after page all the same. Every one was practically illegible, and not because of my dyslexia.

I looked up at Thane, my hands trembling with fury. "What the fuck is this?"

"The file," he said. "It's all I could get."

"How the fuck am I supposed to find out anything about his death with this shit?" I threw the file back at him. Papers fell out and flew everywhere, but I didn't care. I stood and stared him down. "You promised to help me."

He raised an eyebrow, heat radiating more strongly from him with rising anger. "And I did. It wasn't easy to even get that much. Ask your friend to spell the pages to reveal what's hidden or something."

"I don't do magic," Kit piped in.

"You really think the DEA would allow a simple spell

to remove their blackouts?" My voice shook, and I clenched my fists to keep from punching him.

The reaper's face told me he knew what he provided was shit, and he had come anyway—almost like he wanted me to take my anger out on him. Maybe he was a glutton for punishment, too. He didn't bother to respond to my question.

"Why the hell did you even come?" I asked.

"A promise is a promise." He hesitated. "And to warn you both to be careful."

"Oh, *now* you care about my wellbeing?" I scoffed. "Be careful about what, exactly? More reapers who lie and cheat their way out of things?"

Referencing Sophia, the reaper gone rogue who almost got both of us killed, was low even for me. His eyes narrowed, and the darkness grew around him, the shadows receding from the walls to pool at his feet. I was treading dangerous waters, but I didn't care.

"Someone is creating more Risen," he said, "and they're not…normal."

The angry retort on my lips fled with a whoosh of breath. Risen were the dead yet still walking creations of necromancers, a practice I thought had died out long ago. Bodies and missing persons—was this what the two women at the market were talking about?

"What do you mean by not normal?" Kit moved out from behind her desk in sudden interest.

"That's all I can say for now." Thane pulled out his teleportation device and pushed the button. A wavering black circle appeared on the floor. "Just be careful." He met my eyes again, the dark blue of his irises lightening to sapphire as his expression softened for the briefest of moments. And then he was gone.

I turned to glare at Kit. Not that I was mad at her by any means, but I needed to glare at someone, and she would understand. "What a useless waste of an afterlife."

She rolled her eyes and pointed to her bedroom. "Punching bag is in there."

I sighed. "No, I need to run."

I meant it literally. Flying was great for thinking through problems, but I needed to pound out my anger on the pavement first. Blood racing through my veins would clear the headache that rose with my frustration. I was no closer to finding out the truth about Mad's death now than ten minutes ago.

Kit helped me pick up all the scattered papers from the file, then headed to her kitchen. I grabbed my purse and felt my phone buzzing with a message. Colin.

"I realized I didn't tell you how beautiful you looked caught in a moment of surprise," his text read. "Guess you have that effect on me. Free tonight?"

My heartbeat did a little skip. Talk about perfect timing. I typed back, "Plans just cleared up. When & where?"

I grinned and looked up at Kit, who raised an eyebrow at me as she filled a cup of water from the sink. "New guy," I said. "Ran into him yesterday after the sentencing. Literally. Almost fell flat on my ass."

"Your ass would still be anything but flat if you fell on it," she said, giving my backside a quick appraisal.

"Why thank you." My phone buzzed with another message: "8, The Bazaar in South Beach. Can I pick you up?"

I could count the number of real dates I'd been on with one hand, and none of them offered to pick me up. This new giddy feeling was kind of addicting. Too bad it never lasted long. But then, I hadn't ever dated one of the fae. Maybe his magic drew me in. I could get used to that, right?

As much as I'd like to be picked up, I wanted to get ready at my penthouse which meant no visitors. I typed out a reply, "I'll meet you there."

"Human?" Kit asked and took a sip from her cup.

I shook my head. "Fae."

Her eyes widened. "Is that wise?"

"Probably not, but it's better than my other options, which are none." I pouted, which wasn't exactly a good look for me, or anyone over the age of five. She wouldn't judge me for it, though.

"You don't try too hard." She hesitated a moment before adding, "You know the fae aren't exactly known for their empathy or morality."

"I'm well aware, but this guy is oddly different, which is probably a huge red flag, right?" I scrunched up my nose as I tucked my phone away in a back pocket. "Sorry I was a jerk."

She shrugged and returned to her desk, catching my eye as she set down her water cup. "Do me a favor and listen to Thane. Be careful."

I blew her a kiss as I left. "Promise."

After a quick stop to change at my small apartment, which wasn't far from Kit's and The Morning Grind, I headed out on my run. I planned to go from the apartment to my penthouse, which was only about four and a half miles, but it would give me plenty of time to work out some of my frustration and ease the tension building between my temples.

I didn't wear headphones because in my line of business you never knew who would come running up behind you, even in the middle of the afternoon. Instead, I wore a single earpiece for emergencies and then listened to the music of the city. Car horns and bus air brakes mixed together with voices, laughter, and the random blast of music drifting out of restaurants and cafes as I passed. My feet beat a steady rhythm against the sidewalks and sometimes the pavement as I crossed streets, my pulse thrumming in tune with it all.

As I ran, my ponytail swayed behind me and the anger boiling inside my body slowly dissipated. It was hard to stay mad when Dazhbog kissed my skin with his warm rays and Perun caressed my face with his cool breezes. My parents taught us that Slavic mythology developed from human and phoenix relations millennia ago, back before humans even kept a written word.

At that time, phoenixes and other supernatural creatures roamed freely from realm to realm, out in the open. Unafraid of repercussion until humans grew in number to a point that other beings' existence—inhuman beings who didn't reproduce at such high rates—became threatened. It was then that the supernatural Community hid in the shadows or withdrew to other realms completely.

How little humans knew of their world.

I had taken Coral Way for my run today because it had more tree coverage than some of the side streets, and Dazhbog's sun was out in full force, not a cloud in sight. I loved the heat of his sun, but I didn't want to develop any unnecessary tan lines. I might not burn as a perk of my genetics, but I definitely bronzed, and I liked a smooth, uninterrupted caramel look to my skin.

When the street ended at 3rd Ave, I headed east toward the ocean. Alice Wainwright Park would be the perfect detour. This park was one of my favorite places to go after running off some steam. Because it wasn't too close to downtown and the main tourist locations, the people who came here lived in the vicinity or were at least local to Miami.

Shady trees surrounded the park and provided relief from the daytime sun, while palm trees dotted the landscape within from the parking lot to the waterfront. I ran by the playground where children's laughter and shrieks filled the air, past pavilions where families and friends gathered to enjoy an afternoon picnic and barbeque, the mouthwatering scents of pork and fritas nearly stopping me in my tracks.

I kept going, even leaping off the small range of outcropping like I was a kid again, until my shoes hit the sandier ground near the low seawall. I found a palm tree to lean against as it swayed in the salt-filled wind. Panting after the run, I let my heart rate slow and took in the view of the lightly cresting waves. Far off in the distance, the towers of Key Biscayne lined the horizon like tiny dominoes.

I enjoyed the peace and semi-quiet all to myself— basketballs striking the court continued to echo around me in a weirdly soothing cadence—until someone mumbling and shuffling their feet along the sandy earth drew my attention to the left; a homeless man, or maybe a drunk from the look of his ratty hair and disheveled clothes, but he was still too far away to know for sure. Poor guy probably hadn't had a scrub in days, maybe weeks.

A quick, strong wind swept by, stirring the seaweed on the ground and passing the man on its way, bringing with it an awful stench of rotting garbage and old blood that threatened to stick to my nose hairs for hours. Way worse than just the seaweed alone. I crinkled my nose and pulled the top of my shirt toward my nose to hide the smell. As the man stumbled closer, I glanced at him again and his glossy, lifeless gaze met mine for a brief moment before returning to the path in front of him.

"Must… go…" he said in a raspy voice, his hands displaying the bones beneath missing patches of skin and reaching out in front of him. That was what I thought he said, anyway.

Except the Risen shouldn't be able to speak.

CHAPTER 5

Friday Evening

What the… I pushed myself off the palm tree, ready to fight. But the dead man continued to shuffle by me, completely unaware of my existence. That was new. I had only seen Risen once before and not up close like this, but everything I knew about them suggested he should be trying to get a piece of me. Like, to eat.

"M-Must…" he said again.

I tapped my earpiece, the only electronic thing I wore when out on a run. "Kit."

"Here."

"Call the DEA," I said. "There's a Risen at Alice

Wainwright Park." I followed behind him. He wasn't headed toward any of the people, which in and of itself was odd, but I wanted to be ready just in case.

No sound came from my earpiece.

"Kit?"

"You're kidding, right?" she asked, her voice strained.

"Wish I was," I said. "He's not going after anyone, but he's mumbling something and seems intent on getting wherever it is he wants to go."

"Mumbling? You're sure he's dead?"

"I mean, his arms are mostly just bones and he smells like a rotten asshole, but I guess he could just be out for an evening stroll."

"Fuck. Stay with it and keep an eye out for more. We don't know what we're dealing with yet."

"Will do." I tapped the earpiece to end our connection and moved up next to the guy on his right, keeping the ocean on his left and out of anyone else's view.

I glanced at him again, the decaying flesh of his face unmistakable up close. Skin just about hung off his jawbone in ragged strips. I tried not to focus on any other details identifying him as dead, like the wriggling movements of *something* disgusting in his ear. Was this one of the missing people the two women at the market were talking about?

"M... ust... go... ho..." the Risen rasped out as he shuffled.

Must go home? I furrowed my brows, trying to figure out if that was what he meant and why the hell he was so intent on getting there. Anyone still at home would not be pleased with the state of this man's arrival. Unless he meant home to his new master who would welcome him with open arms. I shuddered at the unfortunate imagery that idea provoked.

The Risen typically only had one thought in mind: food. After a necromancer raised the person from the grave, or morgue in most cases, the Risen needed to eat to sustain their half-life state. Half-life wasn't even correct. Risen were mindless, soulless creatures who would feed on anything and everything that came too close.

Two senses fully survived their deaths and were magically enhanced beyond human capabilities: smell to find their prey, and taste to chase it for the rest of their days. Technically, they could see and hear as well, but both of those senses dulled to nearly nonexistent when they rose from the dead.

Because of their insatiable need to consume flesh—as much as they could and as fast as possible—creating Risen was an illegal act of magic unless properly supervised by the DEA. The only reason necromancy was allowed at all anymore was to pull memories from the deceased, and it took a very long time, lots of paperwork, and a whole lot of luck to even be considered. Or maybe all it took was a good blow job.

Either way, memories survived not just in the brain, but also in the bones, which meant the DEA could drag out a request as long as they wanted.

The air around us became thin, and I had an awful thought that the planet's oxygen was being sucked out into space. Before my fantasy proved to be reality, an army of reapers arrived, ready with rope and a muzzle to bring the Risen home with them like a stray dog. Reapers' ability to reflect or repel human attention made it possible to arrive by way of teleportation as they did today, and the humans scattered around the park would be none the wiser.

"Are you Veronica?" asked one reaper as he approached while the rest of the team secured the Risen. Brown hair, brown eyes, slim build. He was fairly average-looking, for a reaper anyway. Death and resurrection seemed to make them all more attractive, taking away or smoothing out their flaws, which was highly unfair considering they were fucking dead. What good did it do them now? At least vampires had fun with their good looks.

"Guilty," I said.

He raised an eyebrow. I guessed it wasn't lost on him that I was a thief. Ex-thief. Maybe… To be determined.

"Did you see any others?" he asked.

Behind him, the Risen growled through the muzzle attached to his face and reached out to grab one of his captors who nimbly turned aside, out of reach. A moment later, the Risen and the rest of the reapers disappeared via teleportation.

"No, but this one kept mumbling something about needing to get somewhere," I said, trying to be helpful.

"The Risen don't speak." He pulled out his t-port device.

"Right, but this one did."

The reaper pushed the button on his device, activating the portal. "I'll be sure to note that in the file. Have a nice evening."

Before I could protest further, he was gone. Heat rose in my cheeks as he disregarded me so easily. He hadn't even bothered to look me in the eye when he brushed my comment off. The fucker's bored tone indicated he most definitely would *not* be noting anything in the file.

Shit. I really did not want to call Thane after my temper tantrum, but I had completely overestimated my status with the agency. Why did I think this guy would listen to me? It wasn't like I worked for them or anything. But maybe I should if they weren't going to take this situation seriously.

Looking out over the waves brushing against the seawall before being called back out to sea, I smiled. Yeah, right. Me, working for the DEA. Now that was a funny thought.

I hadn't gotten dolled up in over a week, not since I attended Dr. Renauldo's party with the intent to steal the jewelry box that gifted its users with a set of angel wings—a fact I didn't know at the time—and then found myself at the top of the DEA's Most Wanted list. But hot damn did it feel good tonight. No gown this time, but I did feel fantastically fabulous in my little black dress and heels.

Chiffon was perfect for a night of unknown happenings, hooked around my neck like a collar before flowing out into an A-line that ended just below my butt. The light fabric would keep me from sweating too much and would also hide the waist strap holding a few knives. But my favorite part of the dress, and maybe one I would get to show off tonight, was with one quick flip of the hook at the collar, the garment would slide right off.

The Bazaar was packed, which wasn't surprising considering it was a world-renowned restaurant run by a culinary icon. I let the hostess know I was looking for someone and gave Colin's name. Without hesitation, she led me straight to his table, passing the strange yet oddly fascinating octopus chandelier on our way. The handsome fae sat in a somewhat secluded corner near the kitchen, and with an up-close-and-personal view of the bookshelf-themed wallpaper.

Things were looking up for a night to remember.

Colin stood and smiled as I approached. "And here I thought you looked beautiful yesterday."

Tucking my clutch under one arm, I allowed him to take my hand and kiss the back of it as he did the day before. Tingles spread from head to toe. Not the same scorching heat as someone else I refused to think about, but a good feeling nonetheless.

"Such a gentleman," I said, taking the seat he pulled out for me. "You clean up pretty nicely yourself."

Nicely was an understatement. I had already noted several women drinking in the fae as if he were the cocktail of the hour. The red highlights in his hair weren't as obvious in the dim light, but the thick, lighter-brown waves did little to keep me from wanting to run my hands through them. His fair complexion made the deep sea-green of his irises pop, though the color shifted as fluidly as the ocean.

He wore a light blue suit, reminding me of the mid-morning sky behind a small veil of white clouds, and a simple white t-shirt beneath the jacket. We were in Miami after all. To top it all off, he wore a pair of white loafers with a distinctive logo near the heel.

"The Dolphins, huh?" I asked as he returned to his seat.

Colin gave an almost embarrassed laugh. "Ah, you saw that, did you? Gotta support my team."

"I wouldn't have pegged you as a sports guy, especially not human sports." I smiled to let him know I was teasing.

"I love this realm and all the perks that come with it."

"No sports in the Otherworld?" I asked, genuinely curious. I knew so little of their culture.

"Not quite the same." He grimaced. "'Sports' to my kind mean more of the blood sport variety, though not as gruesome as the vampiric Blood Trials."

The Blood Trials were a series of gladiator-style battles performed by the oldest and strongest vampires to earn the Master Vampire title. Little was known beyond that, as the events were fiercely guarded and those attending kept a tight lip.

Colin indicated the white wine in front of me. "I hope you don't mind, but I chose something I thought we'd both enjoy."

I lifted my glass and took a sip. The wine was refreshing and crisp—perfect for a late-spring evening in Florida. Or any evening in this hot state. "Have you witnessed one of the Blood Trials?" I asked, fairly certain attendance by another species was forbidden.

"Dear gods, no," he said and shuddered. "Even if I were invited, I would not attend. Barbaric."

"Speaking of barbaric," I said, "what brought you to the DEA yesterday? Not for the sentencing, obviously, unless fashionably late in your world means missing the entire show."

He shifted in his seat. "No, I needed to meet with Adam on behalf of the prince."

As an angel, Adam oversaw all the reapers' activities here in Miami. An archangel to be exact, and he had been in his position for as long as anyone I knew could remember.

In fact, no one knew who the previous archangel managing the reapers had been, if there had ever even been another.

Thankfully, he and I were on good terms after our little escapade through the skies. Well, *good* might have been a stretch, but I preferred to remain optimistic. I didn't know if angels held grudges, but I had proved to be sneakier, if not faster, than him. Then again, he hadn't been pursuing me for real, I just didn't know it at the time.

"Dare I ask why?" I dared.

Colin gave an apologetic look. "You can ask, but I'm not at liberty to say."

"Fair enough. How long have you lived here?"

He pursed his lips as he calculated. "Let's just say longer than you but not as long as some."

"That's entirely unhelpful."

Colin's grin was contagious. "I'm afraid you'll run away screaming if I tell you my real age. Besides, isn't it impolite to ask?"

"Only if you're a lady."

"How sexist." He winked.

The server arrived to take our orders, and Colin allowed me to go first. The perfect gentleman. Something definitely had to be wrong with this guy.

After ordering, the night continued as perfectly as it began. Our food was a gift from the gods, the wine continued to delight and refresh, and the conversation flowed as easily as an ocean breeze. An hour passed in the blink of an eye.

I gave Colin a scrutinizing eye as I lifted my refilled glass. The slight tingling in my head told me I was lubricated enough to get into the nitty gritty. "Okay, so what's wrong with you?"

He let out a small laugh. "Wrong with me?"

"You're too much of a gentleman to be real." I swirled the wine in my cup before taking a sip. Not to mention he hadn't run away from my awkward flirting attempts. Yet. The night was still young.

After setting down his glass, he leaned back in his chair to regard me with amusement. "Well, I'm not human," he pointed out.

I tapped my chin with a finger as if in thought. "Right, but aren't fae supposed to be all brooding and evil, luring humans to bed only to ravage them to death?"

"Call me an anomaly," he said with a wink that made flutters tickle my stomach.

"There's gotta be something else, then." I chewed on my lip. "Did you murder your mother? Kidnap a princess?"

Colin considered both. "Not that I recall, but then, would I tell you the truth if I did?"

"I've heard the fae can't lie."

"You heard right." He grinned, his blue-green eyes twinkling. "So, what's wrong with *you*?"

"All the things."

"I seriously doubt that." His gaze roved over my face and bare shoulders before meeting mine again.

My body warmed with the very welcome visual inspection. Maybe a physical inspection soon, too. I smiled. "I'm a thief."

"Still?"

"Well, no." I sighed. "Now I just help people track down basic lost goods and pets."

"Like a detective," he suggested. "Sounds boring."

Our conversation paused as a server came by to fill up our water glasses before moving on to the next table. When it was just the two of us again, I scrunched up my nose. "Incredibly boring. The most danger I've seen all week was bumping into a Risen earlier today."

Colin stiffened. "You saw a Risen?"

"Yeah, but don't worry," I waved a hand dismissively, "the DEA came and picked it up."

He leaned forward, his eyes intent as he scanned my arms. "Did it hurt you?"

"No, it didn't even seem like it wanted to eat," I said as I recalled the dead man's mumbling. Based on the DEA agent's dismissiveness, I decided against mentioning the mumbling, even if he did meet with Adam. The angel could tell the fae if he wanted. "He just wanted to get somewhere."

"Where were you?" he asked, his voice tight with some kind of emotion—anger? Fear? Neither one expected.

"Alice Wainwright Park," I said, leaning forward to set down my wine glass. "But like I said, it's been picked up and there weren't any others."

He nodded, but his thoughts were clearly distracted. "This is not good."

I reached across the table and laid my hand over one of his. "Hey, it's okay."

Colin snatched his hand away and glanced around the restaurant. He pushed his chair back roughly and stood. "I'm sorry to have to go so quickly, but I need to...to speak with Adam."

I opened my mouth to stop him, but he turned on his heel and pushed through the kitchen door, disappearing from view. I sat there with my mouth hanging open.

What the fuck just happened? Was Colin investigating the bodies and missing persons and now the Risen? Ugh. It would be just my luck to get caught up with yet another attractive man who worked for the DEA. At least it wasn't a failed attempt at flirting that made him run. Or was it?

"Can I get you anything else, miss?" the server's voice startled me out of my thoughts.

"No, thank you, just the bill." I was all about paying my equal share, but getting stuck paying for the entire evening at an expensive restaurant royally pissed me off, even if I did have a fortune to my name.

"Mr. Ó Broin has already settled the bill. Have a lovely evening." The server turned away, leaving me to my confused thoughts once again.

Okay, then. At least I had the rest of the second bottle of wine to myself. I poured the last of it into my glass, filling it nearly to the brim, and downed it all in one go. I grimaced as I set the glass down, regretting my impulsive decision immediately. Wine was not a chugging beverage.

Luckily for me, an arrest for FUI—flying under the influence—didn't exist. I'd had enough of hot, sexy inhuman men leaving me a mess of confused emotions and thoughts. I would swear them off for good.

For tonight, anyway.

CHAPTER 6

Saturday Afternoon

The house was fairly modest—and that was being kind—for being the home of the local werewolf pack's alpha. I had expected a bit flashier, maybe not quite as flashy as Xavier's condominium building, but still more than this block on stilts. But then again, I didn't know that much about werewolves and their preferences for a den.

What I did know was that it was smarter to approach them during the day and not near a full moon. I checked the box on both those accounts with this visit.

Luka Navarro was the resident alpha wolf of Miami and quite a bit of the surrounding area. Despite my client Tabitha's opinion of the man, an opinion I didn't think she believed herself, he had a reputation for being fair but stern. So, like any good father figure. I didn't understand why he would keep her husband's wedding ring from her, but I had a sneaking suspicion he had a good reason. Hopefully I could talk him past that good reason with my charm. If not, well, there was a reason I had turned to thieving in the first place.

After getting out of my car, I stopped before the steps leading to the front stoop. It was way too hot to wear pants, so I had gone for a simple blue blouse on top and closed-toe pumps to seem more official. I waited with my hands tucked casually into my linen shorts pockets. I had called that morning to arrange the visit, but one does not simply waltz straight into a wolf den, invited or not.

As expected, they came out from behind the house to surround me in a loose circle, though still in human form. Deep brown, gold, and green eyes regarded me with the intensity of hunters from all angles. Seven pairs of eyes, unless one came up behind me unnoticed.

I faced the man directly in front of me, holding my head high and removing my hands from my pockets. This wouldn't be Luka, but he would be the beta, the next in line and the second most-powerful wolf of the pack. Because I wasn't a member, I was not expected to show submission, but that didn't stop them from trying to get it.

"Why does the infamous Veronica Neill need to meet with Luka?" asked the beta.

Ooh, I'm infamous now. I like that.

The man's brown eyes flashed gold beneath thick, furrowed eyebrows. A crooked nose, broken too many times without being set properly to heal, marred his face and would keep him from being considered a handsome man by most. Close-cropped dark brown hair, a rich brown hue to his skin, and that melodious Spanish accent that made so many girls swoon would be his saving grace.

Not that he needed to make anyone swoon as the beta of the pack. He had the pick of the litter after the alpha.

"That's between me and Mr. Navarro," I said, my arms remaining loose and unthreatening as the pack closed in around me.

A low growl rumbled behind me, and more than one lip in my periphery raised in a snarl. One young woman with long black hair and a chip on her shoulder stepped close, getting in my face and taking a deep inhale. Her nose almost tickled my chin. She licked her lips as she took a small step back, her eyes lightening to the same yellow-gold as the beta's. Wolf eyes. "I love the smell of fear."

"Oh, honey, if you smelled fear then I think your sniffer is broken." I smiled at her growl but turned my attention back to the beta. "I'm not one of yours to submit and your intimidation tactics won't make me leave. Tell Luka I'm here for my visit."

A few of the younger ones grumbled, probably disappointed they wouldn't get to fight me. Although if I pissed Luka off too much, they might actually get their wish.

The front door opened and a man stepped out onto the stoop, drying his hands on a kitchen towel. My mouth practically fell open to pant like one of the wolves.

The man standing at the door failed to don a shirt before coming out, and my, oh my, did he take care of himself. Beneath rich russet skin, like coffee with just a splash of cream, muscles rippled with every minute movement he made. Washboard abs just barely ended at the low-riding waistline of his jeans. When my gaze finally drifted up, deep amber eyes regarded me with amusement beneath wavy black hair.

Maybe *this* was the reason Tabitha didn't want to come by herself. Could I really blame her? Yeesh.

"I'd give my apologies for the lack of decency," he said, a thick Spanish accent spiking his words, "but I don't think I've offended you."

"No one with abs like that would ever offend me." I stepped past the other wolves, knowing his words to be an invite to me and a dismissal to his pack, and reached out my hand before climbing the steps. I wouldn't submit, but I could show respect. "Veronica Neill."

The beta continued to watch me with narrowed eyes as I approached his alpha. To be expected.

The shirtless man's hand enveloped mine almost completely when he shook it. "Luka Navarro. Come on in." He tilted his head and stepped back to allow me inside. "I nearly lost a battle with a leaky faucet. Let me grab a new shirt."

"Don't bother just on my account," I said cheerfully as I walked up the few steps and over the threshold. He chuckled and closed the door behind us before disappearing around a corner.

The house itself had appeared small on the outside, so it wasn't surprising that the living room was just large enough to hold a two-seater couch, an armchair, and a flatscreen TV on the wall. A floral-patterned sheet covered the couch, and I assumed it was to keep wolf hair off the furniture beneath.

Luka popped back around the corner, pulling a red shirt over his abs. Such a shame.

"To what do I owe the honor of your visit?" He indicated I sit on the chair while he pulled the sheet off the couch, careful to collect any hairs within the sheet before rolling it up.

I sat and crossed one leg over the other. "Tabitha Delgado."

Luka sighed as he sat facing me. "Why did she not come herself?"

"For some unknown reason, you intimidate her." I quirked one of my eyebrows. "All she wants is her husband's ring. A widow's reminder."

"The ring is not hers to have. It belongs to the pack."

"An exception can't be made for a grieving widow?" I pushed. "A single mother?"

He narrowed his eyes at my attempt to guilt him. "No."

"That hardly seems fair."

"Maybe to someone who is not a member of the pack. Tabitha knows the ring remains with the pack until she chooses another mate."

Well, that was interesting. "If it goes to her next husband, why can't she just have it until then?"

The muscles along his chin moved as he clenched his teeth. "It is the way of the pack. She has chosen to remove herself from my safety. When Tabitha is ready to return, we can talk."

I watched the way his features shifted when he said her name. His expression softened, his pupils dilated, and my nostrils flared as his scent changed. Something clicked into place. "You're in love with her."

His eyes met mine, opening wide in startlement. "How could you possibly think that?"

"Honestly, I don't even know," I said, just as baffled. "I'm not usually very good at reading people."

Luka let out a single laugh before his face went dark again. "Her father was our last alpha."

Ah, a complicated love then. Her father must have died in a hunt, or maybe Luka challenged him to become the current alpha, resulting in her father's death or banishment. Either way, she might find it difficult to return Luka's affections, if she was aware of them at all. "Was she married before or after you became alpha?"

He stood. "Listen, Veronica, I can appreciate you coming on her behalf, but this is a pack problem. If she wants to discuss the ring, she knows how to find me."

And that was that. Luka led me to the door and lifted a hand goodbye as calmly as if we just had afternoon tea. The rest of the pack had dispersed, although two continued to watch me from rocking chairs on the front stoop as I made my way back to my car.

The man clearly loved Tabitha, his whole body language gave it away; the question was whether or not she felt the same. Depending on what happened with her father, she might have loved Luka back once. If her father had died on a hunt or of natural causes, then I wasn't quite sure why she would refuse Luka's affections. Looks weren't everything, of course, but damn. Girlfriend would be a lucky lady with that eye candy on her arm.

I pursed my lips in thought as I climbed into my car. There had to be more to it. If he had challenged her father for supremacy, then Tabitha must have chosen a new mate. But had she done so out of heartbreak, or defiance?

As I drove back down the gravel drive toward the main road, I glanced in my rearview mirror. A distant look of sorrow and grief gripped Luka's face, his gaze lost among the trees.

CHAPTER 7

Saturday Night

I felt and looked good. Not just good—hot. My banged-up body had finally finished healing itself, leaving me feeling fresh as a just-bloomed tulip. The short amount of time since my encounter with Xavier was warp speed for any human body but dragged on forever to my supernatural one. The angelic healing provided by my guardian angel Jessa had actually sped it up even faster, but try telling that to my patience.

With Xavier safely behind bars and about to lose his head, the redheaded angel went back to keeping a loose eye on me. That was what she told me she would do, anyway. I was beyond thankful to have her on my side, but no one enjoyed the idea of being watched all the time, even if her lagoon-colored eyes were the most amazing thing ever.

Some of my young, as in just turned twenty-one, co-workers from The Morning Grind convinced me to go out dancing with them that night. For a fleeting moment after they asked, I almost said no, worried that I would be the old hen going out with the young chicks, which might have been a terrible analogy since I didn't have any kids.

Regardless, after meeting with Luka earlier, the need for a drink and a distraction outweighed the worry. And as soon as I got ready and headed downstairs, the excitement came out in full swing.

Because I was feeling feisty after my failed date the night before—a date whom I still hadn't heard from and had since written off—I decided to drive to the club. My Mercedes Benz Maybach, fire-red with a hint of sparkle, always lifted eyebrows, and pulling up in style always lifted my mood.

My previous job as an acquirer had netted me a boatload of cash, and while I didn't spend it extravagantly like some others I knew, I didn't have any problem upgrading my car and my digs (hello, penthouse). And every once in a while, a fancy night out with friends. Sure, I might have acquired said funds by illegal means, but no one was going to show up at my doorstep asking me to return the money. I hadn't stolen the *money,* after all. Plus, they would be hard-pressed to prove anything.

Angels not included, of course, and they would have come knocking long before now had they cared.

Not to mention, I'd survived becoming a Master Vampire's zombie sex slave or broodmare or whatever he had in mind for me, *and* saved a bunch of Community members already enslaved in Xavier's collection. I pretty much earned everything I had with that act alone, right? That was what I kept telling myself to justify it all, and so far it was working just fine.

When the valet opened my door, I stepped out and adjusted my skirt before heading straight for the club's door. The beat of the deep bass within enticed those waiting in line, giving the sense that the wait and the astronomical door fee would be worth it.

I went for a somewhat simple look tonight with an almost knee-length but high-waisted skirt sporting a slit up my right thigh almost to my hip to permit dancing. The fabric stuck to my ass like glue yet still allowed for a small pocket hip for my phone, and a matching sleeveless crop top showed off my toned midriff.

The color of the ensemble was somewhere between midnight blue and lapis lazuli and would make my violet irises pop. Strappy heels topped off the look while also enhancing my sculpted calves. Like most of the clubgoers as well as the under-thirty Miami population in general, I worked out hard on my days off, counted calories every day unless I shifted forms, and wanted everyone to know it. Except for the shifting part.

I hadn't been to a club in what felt like ages, possibly since Mad's death three years ago, but I still knew the bouncer here at N-V. Tyron's six-foot-five frame and hulking muscles usually made him memorable, but then add in the deep black skin and eyes as radiant as the sun, and he was unforgettable. Too bad for me and the other ladies eyeing him, he was gay and his boyfriend was the cutest thing next to fluffy bunnies.

Those gorgeous golden orbs gave me an approving once-over. His deep, smooth-as-butter voice called out as I closed in, "Veronica, what a surprise."

"I know, too long, right?" I lifted up on tiptoes to smooch his cheek, which he still had to lower for me to reach.

"Hope you're ready for some action with that outfit," he said, pursing his lips knowingly.

"Gods, I can only hope so." I laughed. "My bed's been drier than the Sahara Desert." Not exactly true whenever a certain reaper came along in my dreams, but I hadn't had any action between the sheets in much too long for my tastes. A woman's got needs just as much as any man, and a vibrator only did so much.

Tyron grinned and opened the velvet rope. "Go get 'em, girl."

I passed him with a bounce in my step, feeling on top of the world. Nothing was going to bring me down tonight.

The second bouncer opened the door for me, and I stepped inside, immediately feeling like I had been transported to another world. It wasn't even midnight yet, and the club, large enough to house a herd of grazing mammoths, was packed. Even though I couldn't see it due to all the clubgoers, I knew the main bar stood to the right, stretching from the front of the room all the way to the back.

The rest of the first floor enclosed a square-shaped area in the middle for dancing, sunken a few steps below ground to allow the tables and VIP booths lining the walls a perfect view of the dancers. Four columns at each corner held up a second VIP-only level, opened up like a theatre so those lounging like gods above could gaze down on the dancers as well.

The deep beat of the bass thumped down to my core, calling me to dance and sway beneath the strobe lights. I would answer its call, but not yet. First, I needed to make sure my girls were taken care of.

I found my coworkers at the main level VIP table I had reserved for them, deep in a bottle of champagne. Judging by the high-pitched giggles drifting my way, it wasn't their first bottle. Although the majority of the VIP areas were on the second level, I had chosen a booth near the dance floor and the main bar at the back of the club. This way my friends would be close enough to see the eye candy, as well as be seen by said eye candy. The u-shaped booth could easily seat six or squeeze in eight, which meant the four of us would be comfortable on our own or enjoy snuggling with any potential nightly suitors.

The peals of laughter were contagious as I approached.

"Veronica!" Lynn shouted as if I wasn't right in front of her. Her curly blonde hair was pinned up to show off her long, perfectly golden neck.

"Damn, girl." Tory drew the words out as she looked me up and down. "You've been holding out on us."

"You ladies look gorgeous as usual," I said as I slid onto the cushioned black bench next to the tiny yet fierce Serena. All three women had dressed in bright colors and skintight clothing, showing off their curves and toned bodies. Like I said, in Miami, we liked to work hard and party harder.

"How the hell did you afford a VIP table?" Lynn shouted across the table, the booze making her loud moreso than the volume of music.

I laughed. "I saved up."

She gave me a thumbs up and downed the bubbling liquid in her glass. I had some catching up to do. A server dressed in a silver skirt designed a bit like a flapper's dress, with layers upon layers of fringe and a matching bra top, came by to refill our glasses.

I slipped her a few bills. "Keep it coming, please."

She glanced at the money, her eyes widening in surprise before she grinned at me. All set. She sauntered off, the fringes of her skirt swaying and catching the light.

After that, I lost myself in the music and giddy conversation, simply enjoying my life for what it was and for helping my new friends have a night they would talk about for months to come. It had been far too long since I had a night out just for fun without having to worry about a job to finish. Tomorrow I would need to refocus my efforts at uncovering the truth about Maddox's death and figuring out what to tell Tabitha.

But for now, I'd give myself a break. I had earned it, damnit.

Warmth radiated behind me, and the girls went quiet as they stared over my shoulder, their mouths slightly parted.

Fuck. Not tonight.

I turned my head and let my gaze rove over Thane's body the way he always did with mine. As usual, he was much more attractive than anyone had a right to be, and heat surged through me as a result, pooling between my thighs. He had rolled the sleeves of his pale pink button-up shirt to his elbows, allowing everyone a view of his sculpted forearms. The top buttons remained undone, displaying a bit of his hard, bare chest, a gold cross, and a second chain hanging around his neck.

When I raised my eyes to his face, he smirked at me.

"Enjoying the view?" he asked.

"I was enjoying the peace and quiet," I threw back, reliving our very first encounter. Had it really only been two weeks ago?

"May I?" he held out a hand.

I was going to say no, that I was there to get to know my friends better, except Serena practically pushed my ass off the seat. I grabbed his hand out of instinct to keep from falling out of the booth, and internal flames whooshed up my arm from his touch, setting me ablaze in all the best and worst places. This man affected me in a way that no other man—no other person—had ever done.

Thane led me down the few steps toward the dance floor just as the music switched to a modern, faster-paced version of Sway with Me, perfect for a brisk tango.

"Did you plan that?" I asked, pursing my lips.

He winked, sending another molten wave through to my core. "You'll never know."

Then he pulled me close, his cheek brushing mine for a moment, allowing the spicy scent of cardamom to fill my nose and make my mouth water. The warmth of his body all but melted me as we began to dance. His hands moved over my body like he wanted to own it, and I wanted to give it to him. Our eyes met whenever we faced each other, and desire raged just behind his dilated pupils.

He pulled me close again, my back against his chest as we swayed for a moment. Breathing onto my neck and tickling the hair along my skin, he lowered his lips to gently caress my bare shoulder. This time, a sweet bergamot drifted around me with his embrace, his scent changing with his mood. I tilted my head back, eyes closed, letting go of the dance for a moment, just wanting to lose myself in his touch. Then he swung me out as the beat picked up once again.

We danced, the world around us falling away. I'd never had such a capable partner, someone who understood and embraced the beat as well as I did. Dancing had been a part of my life as long as I could remember, until Maddox died. I had let go of a lot of things I used to enjoy then, and it felt incredible to relive my passion for the art. I gave myself to the tango, to him, forgetting everything that had happened over the last two weeks.

As the song ended on the final, abrupt note, he bent me backward over his arm, my blonde hair tumbling down toward the floor. My heart beat wildly in my chest, both from the physical exertion as well as the thrill of his fingers inching their way up my bare thigh.

His other hand slid slowly up my back to help me stand until our faces were a mere inch apart and sparks practically flew between us. The scorch of his touch remained on the back of my neck, and I knew he was going to kiss me.

Fucking finally.

CHAPTER 8

Saturday Night

My chest rose and fell with my heavy breathing, and my arms glistened from the heat of the club as I ran my hands up the front of Thane's shirt. His eyes burned with desire, silver specks dancing around his deep blue irises like fish in the sea. This was the first time I truly knew he wanted me the way I did him. The feeling was more than just a man and a woman attracted to each other by pheromones and lack of sex (at least on my part).

An underlying sense of destiny saturated our every moment together, and I was ready to give in.

Applause and whistles erupted around us, snapping me back into the reality of where I was and who I was with—a fucking reaper who toyed with my emotions. I took a shaky step back from Thane before dipping into a wobbling curtsy for the crowd. Without waiting for him to follow, I strode off the dance floor and straight toward the bar. Strands of my hair stuck to my neck and shoulders.

I needed a fucking drink. Destiny, my ass. I would have blamed my delirious thoughts on alcohol except I hadn't had nearly enough to even give me a buzz. It was time to fix that. I nudged my way through the crowd milling around the closest bar until I got to the counter and flagged down the bartender.

"Great performance," she said, flashing me a grin. Sweat shone on her toned, near-naked body from the heat of the club and having to run back and forth behind the bar all night. "What can I get you?"

"Tequila. A double, please."

"1942 or Clase Azul?"

"1942."

"Coming right up." She tilted her gaze up and behind me, a smirk on her lips. "Anything to put that fire out?"

Thane stood behind me, of course. I didn't need anyone to tell me; I could feel his heat swirling around me, making me dizzy.

"I'm good, thanks," he said.

If the women ogling him were any indication, he wasn't here in his enforcement or reaping capacity, which meant he didn't repel humans' attention away from him after the dance. His goddamn sex appeal only drew the hyenas in closer.

The bartender winked at me and turned around to face the bottles.

Thane pushed through the throng to reach the space next to me and leaned an arm on the bar top. Dazhbog above, I wanted this man, and I couldn't explain it even to myself. Most men did one of three things around me: avoided me altogether, tripped over their own shoelaces in their attempt to approach me, or tried some arrogant, douchey pick-up line.

Thane had done none of those things. Maybe he was older than he looked, and he had the experience under his belt. Probably not, though. I didn't know how long he had been a reaper, but my guess was not too terribly long if his mother still kept his apartment in the hopes his spirit would visit it. Whatever age he was, he somehow knew exactly how to approach me and with such finesse that I couldn't resist. Or maybe I was just a bigger sucker than I realized.

The bartender dropped off my double shot of tequila and gave me a wink. "On the house, love."

I downed the shots in a single gulp, and my eyes somehow found his as I set the shot glass back on the counter. Next to the fire he induced inside of me, his looks didn't matter that much—they were just the icing on the mouthwatering cake he presented. The deliciously juicy cherry on top.

He smirked, his full lips pulling up at one corner. "That bad, huh?"

"Thirsty."

"Quenching your thirst with tequila could have unintended consequences." His fingers trailed up my arm, leaving a searing burn behind.

I couldn't help it, I shivered. "Why are you here?"

His hand dropped but the heat remained, tingling

through my skin. "I need your help on a case."

Varying emotions crashed through me like a tidal wave. He had sought me out tonight to ask me to work with him? Part of me was thrilled at the idea, and I almost licked my lips in anticipation. Even though my life had been on the line, tracking down the real killer of the fae duke had been exhilarating, especially with Thane tagging along.

But the other part of me, and the part that was slowly crushing the other like a bug underfoot, was furious. I turned away from him, trying to hide the flush that rose in my face. He had only shown up tonight to get my help, even though he completely failed to provide any real success with my brother's file. Not only that, but he swept me up into a fantasy with that perfectly executed tango, and he *knew* I would fall for him all over again.

Gods, was I that predictable?

And then I grew even angrier when I realized I royally sucked at reading men. I crumpled the napkin beneath my shots in one hand, clenching the paper tight. I wanted to say my recent poor choices came from being attracted to inhuman men, reapers and fae alike, but it shouldn't have mattered. *I* was inhuman. Shouldn't I have a better heir-producer-picker? Like survival of the fittest and all that?

The sacred mating ritual of the phoenix used magic that wouldn't survive outside my body if I tried to procreate via science, which meant I couldn't even have a future with the reaper if I wanted my species to continue. Nothing more than a casual dalliance. So why was I letting him get to me so bad?

"You still with me?" his voice cut through my thoughts.

Fuck it. I slammed the crushed napkin down on the

counter. "What case?"

He eyed me for a moment. "The Risen."

I glanced around as the noise of the bar and crowd dulled to a minor buzzing. The women eyeing Thane as their next meal had turned their attention elsewhere, and he now had a sizable space around him as others moved away subconsciously. Reaper repellant engaged. He could bend me over backward across the bar top, take me right then and there, and none would be the wiser.

This was such a bad idea.

My head felt thick with unquenched desire, but I licked my salty lips and focused. "What about the Risen?"

"Well first off, they keep popping up, as you discovered." He gave me a knowing look as if I should have called him instead of anyone else.

I gazed back at him with doe eyes, batting my eyelashes dramatically.

"Second," he said, "they're not…normal."

I let out a surprised laugh. "You said that before, but are Risen ever considered normal?"

"These new Risen are aware. Almost intelligent. They've been given a specific task and they want nothing more than to complete it."

Goosebumps spread along my body. I had seen exactly what he described. "What is the task?"

"We don't know yet. That's what I want your help to figure out."

I narrowed my eyes. "Why me? I'm sure you agents have all kinds of fancy tools and insider information to help you. *Files* galore."

He sighed. "I'm sorry, Veronica."

My heart skipped a beat. "What was that? I think I misheard."

"I'm sorry the file wasn't what you expected, but I can get you the whole, unedited file this time if you help me track down the necromancer responsible."

"Adam agreed to that?" And also, why the hell didn't he do it the first time if he could do it this time?

He smirked. "Adam doesn't know I'm here, but he'll agree if we figure this out. This is too big of an issue."

I raised an eyebrow at him. "Don't tell me you're going rogue now, too."

"I enjoyed working with you." Thane took my hand, entwining my fingers with his. Sparks should have been flying with the amount of heat produced with his touch. "You're…addicting."

My stomach dropped to the floor. As much as I hated to do it, I pulled my hand free at his choice of words. "Is it such a smart idea to work with me considering you died of an overdose?" I wasn't trying to be mean, but I also didn't like how his comment made me feel. Like I was his next drug of choice.

"I didn't mean it like that," he said, frowning. "I enjoy your presence."

I was such a sucker, I believed him. Butterflies did a little happy dance in my stomach. "Fine. I'll help you, but only if I get the real file this time."

"Deal." He held out his hand, and I laughed. A reaper's word was as good as they came, even if they always managed to find loopholes.

I swatted away his hand. "Tell me what you know about these Risen so far."

"I can do better than that," he said, a gleam in his eye. "I can show you."

"Ew. Show me what, exactly?"

He rolled his eyes. "The bodies. We have them at the morgue. Seeing them would go a lot farther than trying to explain it."

I crinkled my nose as I remembered the dead man on the beach. "Do I have to? Technically, I already saw one."

"I thought you were a badass thief." The side of his lip quirked up.

"Stealing doesn't require a strong stomach like murdering must. If you'll recall, I wouldn't know. But I am still a badass, and you better not forget it."

"There's more to the bodies you need to see."

I glared at him. "You're going to make me, aren't you?"

"If you're going to help, yes."

"Then I want something else out of our little deal."

He chuckled. "What's that?"

I thought for a moment, not actually having anything planned. I just figured if I had to go look at a Risen's dead, decaying body up close—I shuddered at the thought—then I wanted more from this whole arrangement. But what the hell did I want?

"A date." The words were out of my mouth before I could stop them.

Fuck. Was I really bribing a DEA agent to date me? Had I gotten so desperate?

"Only if it's with me." He grinned.

My heart did a little jump. "Only if you're lucky. I get to pick the guy."

He moved closer, reaching a hand up to brush my hair

back from my cheek before tracing the line of my jaw with his fingers, leaving tingles in their wake. He leaned his head in, trailing his lips back along the line he had traced on my jaw, branding me with each subtle kiss as he moved toward my ear.

My body quivered, desperate to have those lips moving down my neck and across my breasts. I pressed myself against him, rewarded with the undeniable feel of his arousal.

His lips moved against my cheek as he whispered, "I guarantee you won't want anyone else once I have my way with you."

"Veronica!" Tory's voice cut through the moment. "There you are."

I didn't know if I wanted to hug or slap her at that moment. She and the other two were pushing their way through the crowd to get to me.

My body shuddered with an unsatiated craving as Thane took a step back, his eyes blazing with a similar hunger.

"Meet me tomorrow. I'll message you," he said and turned around. The crowd parted around him to allow him through without even noticing his presence.

"That guy you danced with is so fucking hot," Serena said. "Is he your boyfriend?"

I took a deep breath to calm my racing heart. "Not even close."

"Don't tell me you don't want that fine piece of ass," Tory said, looking around for him.

With his reaper ability engaged, they hadn't caught that steamy moment between us. Thankful didn't even come close to how I felt knowing they hadn't witnessed me about to give myself to him right then and there.

I honestly didn't know what I wanted from Thane. As the girls interrogated me for the next few minutes about where I had learned to dance like that and who the mystery man was and every detail in between, my thoughts remained scattered.

Obviously, I physically wanted the man, dead or not. There was no denying the unbelievable chemistry between us. But I wasn't sure it was such a smart move to keep flirting with fire this way. I had been burned by a man before—not quite like this, of course, but it was not a pretty clean up. There was no way anything between Thane and I would end well, and Kit would kill me if she had to pick up the pieces of my shattered heart again.

But why was I so focused on dating the reaper? Maybe if we just did the deed and got it out of our systems, we could move forward without distraction. That sounded much smarter.

Except for one thing.

I knew deep down that sleeping with Thane would only ignite a stronger flame—an inferno that nothing could put out.

I was fucked, just not the way I wanted to be.

CHAPTER 9

Sunday Morning

As promised, Thane texted me with the details for where to meet him and when. That motherfucker had requested my presence at the morgue at eight in the morning on a Sunday after a night at the club. If he wasn't already dead, I might have killed him.

The only reason I didn't was because I actually wanted to be in on this case, and alcohol metabolizes faster in my blood than a human's. Okay, so two reasons I didn't kill him that morning. But in all honesty, after working with just two clients in my new gig as a sort of pseudo-supernatural private investigator, I was ready for some real adventure. A little danger. Something to spice up my time more since I kept failing miserably on the man front.

I decided not to shift and fly to our appointment because I didn't want to deal with getting hungry at the morgue—that was just a little too macabre for my tastes—so I took out my Mercedes again. The sun was already beginning its ascent into the sky, blue from horizon to horizon, and the humidity was as thick as ever. Xavier's head would be rolling on the floor the next morning, and I was working on something a little more exciting than convincing an alpha werewolf to return a husband's wedding ring to his widow.

So, in my book, it was a perfect start to the day. I put the top down on my convertible and drove with the wind chasing my ponytail.

According to our legends, my kind came directly from the sun. A pure celestial lineage. Dazhbog, our creator and lord of the sun, sculpted us from the star's flames and made us immune to both fire and heat in general. I still felt the heat of the sun but only as a gentle, loving caress across my skin.

I didn't know why we were the last phoenixes, or why Dazhbog would allow that to occur. But as a rebellious teen, I hadn't cared enough to ask, and now the people who might have known were gone. Besides, I felt like Dazhbog made sure my close encounters never resulted in a true death. Not quite a guardian angel like Jessa, but always there.

Downtown Miami still hadn't woken up by the time I turned onto the street leading into the DEA office's parking garage. Only early birds like me would be out before eight o'clock on a Sunday. I passed a woman out for a run, a man walking his dog, and a window washer before I entered the garage. Three whole people. The other cars didn't count as a reliable sign of busyness in my book since the roads were always busy, but there weren't a lot of those, either.

Thane met me at the door that led into the DEA building. I had chosen leggings that morning because, while the heat didn't bother me, cold definitely did. I knew morgues were kept at fairly chilly temperatures, and wearing shorts around bodies just felt weird somehow. Disrespectful. I pulled on a zip-up hoodie as I approached the reaper, who was wearing his everyday business clothes—a button-down with the sleeves rolled up to his elbows and crisp slacks.

Even with my layers of clothes, his eyes appraised my body, roving over my curves. He had already seen me in some compromising positions—not sex of course, I had just passed out a time or two in front of him and woken up in my silk pajamas, totally awkward—so I imagine he saw more of me in his memories than my clothes today revealed. The pervert.

"You're not a morning person, are you?" he asked when I reached him.

Or maybe he had been judging my comfortable, just-rolled-out-of-bed look more than imagining me naked. The bastard.

"Only the dead don't need sleep." I gave him a pointed look.

Thane smirked. I guessed he had gotten past whatever insecurity used to rile him up when I cracked dead jokes, and it also seemed neither of us would be discussing last night's steamy moment at the club. If he wasn't going to bring it up, I certainly wouldn't either. He held the door open behind him, allowing me in. I brushed past him into the stairwell, the brief heat of his body seeping through the layers I wore.

The last time we had been in the garage together, I had just broken him out of his holding cell with the help of my fantastic partner in crime, Kit. We had faced down a group of reapers, his coworkers as well as the real killer in the crime inaccurately pinned on us, and then fled.

"Adam didn't have anyone clean up the burn marks?" I asked before he closed the door, indicating the scorched garage ceiling and the crack through the floor where my fiery lance had melted through the concrete.

Thane grinned. "He said it's a good reminder that we need to always remain vigilant and keep our security systems up to date."

"You're welcome," I said with a nonchalant shrug, though in reality I was feeling pretty damn smug inside. Adam was definitely growing on me, but I had no idea if the feeling was mutual.

I followed Thane down a level to the morgue. There was parking on that level, too, since it was where they brought in the bodies, but I had a feeling the reaper wanted me to see the burn marks still there. I just didn't know if he was doing it for fun or to warn me not to attempt a break-in again. Not that I would listen to the warning if I needed to get into the building, of course.

As predicted, it was cold in the morgue. Not cold enough to see my breath fog out in front of me, but I wouldn't have been totally surprised if it had. A young, blond man a few inches taller than me and wearing a white lab coat met us in the entryway, a clipboard held in one arm. Blue eyes twinkled at me behind wire-framed glasses and gave me the sense this reaper was much older than he appeared.

"Veronica, meet Dr. Owen Cooper, the DEA's lead mortician here in Miami," Thane said.

I put out my hand. Owen grinned and shook it exuberantly. "The legendary Falcon. So brave. Most people are too leery to shake my hand."

My skin prickled. Had I just made a terrible faux pas? "Why?"

"Because I work on cadavers with these hands." He wiggled his fingers for emphasis.

"But you wear gloves, right?" Sun and sky, I hoped he did.

"That is the question." He winked. "You'll find out soon enough."

I honestly couldn't tell if he was kidding or not, which was highly unnerving, but he motioned for us to follow him down the hallway. The tapping of our shoes echoed against the linoleum floor, the sound competing for dominance against the heartbeat in my ears. Being here was bringing up some memories I wished would stay suppressed.

"We now have three bodies including the one you just found," Owen explained as he walked. "As far as we know, the first one didn't actually Rise, but should have."

"Why do you think it was going to?" I asked as he opened a door and ushered us through.

A large window covered the wall on my right, displaying a small room on the other side with wide swinging doors and two pedestals decorated with pots of fake ferns. The room where he must wheel bodies into view for identification from family members. Across from the window sat a few wooden chairs and a small couch covered in a blue fabric that looked easy to wipe clean. Two heavy swinging doors hung straight in front of us.

For a brief moment, I couldn't breathe. The image of Maddox's face on the other side of a similar window came crashing back—an image I tried to forget but never truly would. His face had looked so peaceful, as if he were only sleeping and would come to at any moment and laugh at the great prank he just pulled. I wouldn't have even grounded him for it because I would give anything, *anything,* for it to have all been some stupid teenage prank.

Because I had tried to shield him, both of us, from this supernatural world after our parents left, he had gone to a human morgue instead of this Community one. Unfortunately, they appeared to be designed the same no matter the location or species.

I gritted my teeth as I stood spellbound. As soon as I got the file, the *real* file, I would know who was responsible for taking my brother from me, and that someone was going to wish to whatever god he or she prayed to that they had never even seen Mad's name.

"All three bodies bear the same necromantic markings." Owen's words broke through the memory, shattering its hold on me. He headed for the swinging doors. "That makes me believe Rising was intended."

I pushed my memories back into the deepest corner of my mind and shut the metaphorical door. Focusing on the here and now, I followed Owen through a door, Thane at my heels.

Never having studied necromancy, I didn't know what marks Owen was talking about. It felt gross to admit, but I was eager to learn more about the world's darkest magic, even though it meant seeing dead bodies that had already started to decompose. Vampires went into their undead life willingly, at least in the modern era, even signing a contract before it could occur. The Risen weren't so lucky, if you could even call becoming a vampire lucky. Yuck.

The autopsy room was all stainless steel and white and even colder than I thought it would be. Every wall, the floor, and even the ceiling were painted blindingly white, as if the color would somehow banish any lingering spirits back to the awaiting dark. Square metal lockers covered one wall, latches keeping each door from swinging open. Those would be the fridges where the bodies were kept.

Owen stopped at a counter and handed us a tub of Vicks VapoRub. "Smear a little under the nose. The smell won't be too bad since they've been on ice all night, but it's best to be prepared."

We did as told, then he handed us each a pair of latex gloves. I definitely would not be doing any touching, but I didn't argue. The gloves were like an added layer of protection for keeping my jittery nerves in, made even worse by the chilly temperature. I was relieved to note Owen did in fact wear gloves.

"Nervous?"

I jumped at Thane's unexpected voice behind my ear and whirled to glare at him. I hadn't even noticed his warmth creeping up on me. "Not nervous, just…fascinated. I haven't seen this side of magic before."

The reaper flashed another one of his rare grins, a real smile that made it all the way up to his eyes. "You've seen plenty of the previously dead now."

I rolled my eyes and turned my back on him and his luscious lips, ignoring the thumping of my heart that had nothing to do with the room or the Risen we were about to see.

The doctor walked to one of the steel lockers, flipped the latch, and opened the door. A small bit of steam licked the air as the freezing temperature inside met with the marginally warmer air in the room. I wouldn't call it warm by any stretch of the imagination but certainly more so than in the actual freezer. Owen pulled the sliding tray out of the locker, revealing the blanketed body.

Goosebumps raced up my arms. This was it.

"We'll start with the one you found," the doc said, "then show you the difference between this one and the first."

Thane furrowed his brows as he stepped closer. "What do you mean? I thought you said they had the same markings."

"Oh, they do," Owen chuckled. "You'll see. First things first."

He flipped the blanket over and I gasped.

CHAPTER 10

Sunday Morning

There was no real way to prepare for seeing a dead body cut open. This wasn't my first time—Broderick's open chest and broken ribs still seared through my memories at the most inconvenient of times—but it didn't appear to get any easier. The only saving grace here was that Owen had sewn the man back together again.

Bile rose in my throat, but I swallowed it down, wincing from the burn and bitter taste the acid left behind. This wasn't some horrific soul-stealing hack job. These cuts had been made by a medical professional determined to tell the story of this man's death. I could do this. But I was also super glad I had chosen not to eat yet that morning.

Owen gave me a sympathetic look. "I forget to warn people sometimes."

"I'm not sure it would have helped," I said.

"True. Let's get started, then." Owen and Thane slid the tray holding the body onto a rolling table, which we wheeled into the middle of the room for better visibility.

The Risen on the slab was definitely the man I saw on the beach, except now his closed eyes and still face looked at peace, almost serene. He had found his final rest. I forced my eyes downward toward his chest, where the markings were.

A very sharp, precise knife had etched symbols into his flesh, approximately two inches by two inches and deep enough to be clearly defined. Except for being kind of pretty with loops and swirly ends, I had no idea what each was supposed to be. Making such clean cuts must have taken quite a bit of talent or lots of practice.

I hoped for the former, but my grumbling gut told me I was likely wrong.

"Were these made before or after he died?" I asked.

"In this man's case, both."

I grimaced. Poor guy.

Thane was all business, walking around the table slowly as he took in every detail. His eyes, a blue so deep they were almost black in this room, narrowed under his still furrowed eyebrows. "Do you know what the markings mean?"

"Nope, that's what you guys are for," the doc said almost cheerfully.

"You have pictures of them?"

"Print or digital?" Owen walked toward the computer in a corner of the room.

"Let's start with digital for now," Thane replied, his eyes never leaving the body.

"Have you seen these symbols before?" I asked, leaning in closer to inspect them. Although at first glance each one seemed to have a somewhat sporadic placement, now I picked out a vague pattern. If I had to make a guess, I would say the marks were some kind of arcane language. They must have told a story of resurrection, just like his Rising had.

Thane shook his head. "We've only had a handful of practicing necromancers the entire time I've been with the agency. This is the first time I've worked on one of the cases."

"How do they learn what to carve? Do they have a Creating Risen 101 textbook or something?"

He shot me an amused look. "Doubtful. I'm not well-versed yet on their training practices, but I know that each necromancer carves their own symbols. It ties the body to them."

I frowned. "I thought they were mindless. Besides this guy, I mean."

"They are, but the mage still maintains a mild control over his creation. The Risen will always seek out its master if separated. Albeit very slowly and leaving more bodies in its wake."

Repressing a shudder, I thought back to the beach. "So that's what he was trying to do? Get back to the necromancer?"

"Most likely," Thane said. "They just don't normally tell you that's what they're doing."

I glanced down at the body, suddenly wary. "Why isn't he trying to get there now?"

"The bond has been severed." Owen popped up at my side, making me jump.

My heart pounded wildly in my chest, and he was lucky I stopped my fist from connecting with his face. It was like these reapers got a kick out of spooking others. Or maybe just me. Keeping the infamous Falcon from getting too big of a head and all that.

"Severed?" I asked when I could form words again.

"As soon as the Risen got here, the necromancer who created him cut the cord, so to speak." Owen made a snipping motion in the air with his fingers. "It keeps us from tracking him down."

Interesting. So if we could catch one still walking, and apparently now talking, and track the perp's magic back, then we could catch the mage responsible.

Sounded simple. Too bad nothing was ever as simple as it sounded in my world.

"Now for the fun part," Owen said, walking toward another locker.

I glanced at Thane, who seemed amused. Fun and dead bodies did *not* mix. At least not the truly dead kind.

Owen opened the locker and pulled out a tray with another body on it. He beckoned us closer, then flipped the covering over to reveal the woman's chest and pointed to the markings. "This was the mage's first, as far as I can tell. You can see how much more confidence he's gained from this body to the other."

I scrunched up my nose. He was right about that. These mutilated symbols had been all but hacked into her flesh rather than precisely defined. No talent, just lots of practice. There was something else different about the two bodies, but I couldn't place my finger on it. I caught Owen watching me carefully.

"You can sense it, can't you?" he asked quietly.

Thane glanced at me. "What?"

I walked back to the other body, the one I had stumbled upon, my mouth parting in shock. "This man was part of the Community. A shifter."

Thane's head whipped back like he had been slapped. "How do you know?"

I shook my head, unable to answer. I didn't actually know how I knew, I just did. The sense of otherness about him was far weaker now than if he were truly alive. I hadn't even picked up on it when he was shuffling down the beach. "Why would the mage raise a shifter?"

"Getting ballsy, I would guess." Owen shrugged. "That or this man was in the wrong place at the wrong time. Or the necromancer may not have known what he was. Not many humans have the ability to detect the inhuman, not even mages."

Thane continued to look between me and the shifter on the slab. He had asked a fair question. How *did* I know? I had always been able to detect the supernatural type when in close proximity, and to be honest, I thought we all could. Being able to detect others was like wearing underwear—I assumed we all did it, but I didn't ask anyone about it.

But the more important question was why did the necromancer raise a shifter? That was just asking for trouble. There weren't many examples to go off of, but the ability to shift stopped in the undead vampire life, so I would assume it did the same when Risen. But assuming only seemed to get me in trouble.

"Can a Risen shift?" I asked, glancing between Thane and Owen for an answer. I wasn't sure if either of them even knew.

"I should hope not," Owen said with a shudder while Thane continued to frown at the body.

After the doctor slid the bodies back into their respective freezers, we retreated to the viewing room, a laptop and files spread out on the table. Owen went back to his work, and Thane and I spent the next few hours digging through all the medical notes on the three recently Risen, as well as over the last couple of years.

Three in one week turned out to be a *lot* more than average.

CHAPTER 11

Sunday Afternoon

Just before noon and not finding out anything that would help our case just yet, Thane and I returned to the parking garage.

"So, where to next?" I asked, my stomach growling. Unlike the reaper, who probably hadn't even considered my needs as a living individual, I'd need to grab a bite to eat at some point in the near future.

"There's an ex-necromancer who lives out in the everglades," Thane said, pulling out his phone. "I contacted him earlier, and he agreed to speak with us."

"Drive or teleport?" My phone buzzed, and I glanced at the screen, my stomach flipping over when I saw who called. "Be right back."

I took a few steps away from Thane and answered Colin's call. "Didn't expect to see your name pop up again."

The fae who had wined, dined, then ditched me sighed, genuine remorse in the sound. "I can't apologize enough for my rude behavior and subsequent silence. Things have been tense."

"So why are you calling?"

"To see if you'll let me apologize in person as a do-over of our date. One more chance before you cut me off for good."

I smiled, tingles spreading from my belly to my toes. A distraction from all the death, Risen and reaper alike, would be lovely. Besides, who was I to judge him too harshly? "I'm feeling generous."

Colin let out a laugh, sending a little flutter through my insides. "Tomorrow? Dinner?"

"Can't. Let's try lunch." I had to at least pretend I had dinner plans.

"I'll make it happen and text you with a location," he said. "See you tomorrow, beautiful."

I stared at my phone after we ended the call, a giddy smile still plastered on my face.

"Who was that?" Thane interrupted my reverie.

"No one you need to worry about." I tucked my phone into my pocket. Part of me wanted to see if I could make the reaper jealous, but the other part of me that won out—for now—wanted Colin to be my little secret until I knew where it was going, if anywhere. No sense in getting my hopes up by telling people if we were just going to part ways.

His eyebrow twitched like he wanted to ask more, but

he pointed to my car instead. "Let's go. We can grab you some food on the way."

Okay, so maybe he *had* considered my needs. That, or he heard my stomach grumbling. I almost let him drive so I could eat like a normal person, but the Benz was the closest thing to a baby I had. No one got behind the wheel but me. We took a quick detour through a drive-thru for a burger before heading west into swamp country—the Everglades.

The man we were meeting operated an airboat company as a tourist attraction. I had never actually been out on one before, despite having spent my entire life right next to the everglades. Today wasn't the day for it, but I added a mental note to try the activity sometime, maybe as a future date idea. It had always looked like fun.

I parked in the back of the lot, not even bothering to see if there was a random, lucky spot closer. Sunday afternoon meant weekend tourists were out in droves. After getting out of the car, I brushed burger bun crumbs from my hoodie before removing the whole thing and leaving it behind. The thick air of the swamps was more than enough to keep me warm in a tank top, not to mention being close to the reaper.

"You sure he's a retired necro?" I asked as we hiked across the dirt and gravel lot toward the main entrance. Mangroves and cypress trees vied for height around the sides of the building before opening up to allow water to flow by behind the structure. An abundance of swaying river grasses at the trees' bases encouraged tourists from wandering too far. "Maybe he snatches a person or two from this motley crew."

I was only kind of joking about the retired necro part,

but the men, women, and children of all ages and all walks of life milling about definitely fit the bill of a motley bunch.

"I'm sure," Thane said, though he glanced around as if I had made some grand point. "As part of his parole agreement, he had to agree to a tracker like mine."

"So the person we're after doesn't have a track record," I said. "Or at least hasn't been caught and prosecuted yet."

He nodded. Reapers all came equipped with a tracking device embedded in the back of their necks. I had seen one in person when Kit helped Thane take his out after we broke him out of the DEA's holding cell. It made sense that some of their parolees had the devices, too. Knowing that tidbit settled my nerves a bit.

The building we entered was the typical tourist trap, filled to the brim with knickknacks and whatchamajigs, all stamped with the park's gator-themed logo. We pushed our way through the forest of so-called gifts and the humans browsing them like prized possessions until we reached the customer service corner.

"We're here to see Frank Turner," Thane told the girl at the desk.

She picked up the phone and made a quick call before pointing us toward a side door. I followed Thane inside the compact office, which was empty other than a simple desk, chair, and small, ancient box-shaped computer. Another door stood open across the room, leading out onto a covered porch overhanging the murky swamp water.

Outside, a man sat in one of two rocking chairs, a cigar held comfortably in one hand. A small, square fold-up table stood between the two chairs, holding an ashtray. Even while sitting, his frame was short and stout, his feet barely brushing the floor. He wore a wide brimmed straw hat, khaki shorts, and a t-shirt sporting the shop's logo and serious sweat stains under a cargo-style vest.

The man couldn't have been more than fifty or so, but he grew a thick, grey beard that matched his long hair, and his skin had definitely seen better days. Sun had scorched patches into a tough leather, but only the parts that regularly saw the light of day. When he moved, the contrast with his lily-white upper arms was evident.

He brought the cigar to his lips and took a puff before realizing we were there.

"Oh, hey," he said, waving us over. "I only got the one other chair, but I don't s'pose you'll be stayin' for a long chat, anywho."

I couldn't tell whether his hillbilly accent was real or if he laid it on thick for the job. Either way, it was disarmingly charming. Almost made me forget who and what he truly was. Sneaky little ex-necromancer.

"Frank," Thane said as he leaned against the railing, leaving the chair for me like a true gentleman. "This is my associate Veronica Neill."

Frank reached out a hand toward me without getting to his feet. "Lucky man." He winked at me.

I shook his hand, noting the tingle that spread across our joined palms. Necromancers were all mages, humans who had learned to bend magic to their will. In theory, I wouldn't feel a thing if he was no longer using magic because he was human. I only sensed otherness. That tingle made me unsure he didn't still cast a spell or two.

"So, how can I help the fine folks at the DEA?" Frank asked, taking another drag of his cigar. He blew out the smoke into thick rings that drifted out over the water and left a pleasing cedar-and-nutmeg scent behind.

"One of your kind is practicing again," Thane said.

"What makes you think they ever stop?" Frank grinned.

"We've snagged three Risen so far. In a week."

He whistled. "That's fast for anyone. I still don't know how you expect me to be of any help."

"We need your contacts," Thane said. "Any and all who were practicing or showed an interest."

Frank's eyes shifted between us. "I've already given you people everything."

"We both know that's not true." The reaper smiled, though there was no warmth behind it.

"Sorry, I can't help you more." Frank dropped the butt of his cigar in the ashtray and rose from his chair. The top of his head barely came up to the reaper's chest. "If you'll excuse me, I've got a tour waitin' on me."

"We're not done yet," Thane said, his tone dipping low into an icy threat that made my skin tingle with unease.

"Ma'am." Frank tipped his hat in my direction before facing the reaper, his lips pressing into a thin smile. "Unless you're here for my soul, *reaper*, get the fuck off my property."

He breezed past me and into the office, leaving Thane and I alone on the porch. The door leading back into the tourist shop slammed shut a moment later, rattling the rafters all the way outside.

"Well, that didn't go well." I glanced at Thane who had pulled out his phone. "Want me to go snoop around his office?"

The side of his lip twitched like he wanted to smirk, though his eyes remained fixed on his phone. "I got what I needed."

"Which is what exactly?"

"He removed his tracking device. But we're still tracking movements close by, which means he put the device into someone else. Maybe some*thing*."

I shuddered. "That's gross. Who would be willing to do that for him? If it's not an alligator or a walking dead body, I mean."

"*Who* isn't that important, it's why Frank felt the need to remove it to begin with." He ran his free hand through his hair as he tucked his phone back into his pocket. "He knows more than he's admitting."

"So, you're arresting him, right?"

Thane shook his head. "I'll get someone to watch him. He could very well lead us straight to the mage responsible, especially if we've spooked him."

Oh, that was a smart idea. Good thing the reaper knew what he was doing. Maybe I would learn a thing or two about understanding people better if I stuck around him long enough. The thought made me smile.

I followed Thane back the way we came and through the gift shop. A prickling sensation skittered along my neck as if we were being watched. I turned around, but everyone was busy shopping, laughing, or ringing someone up. No one was watching us, yet someone definitely was.

"I sense it, too," Thane murmured, but his hand on my arm kept me moving toward the door leading out. When we made it to the parking lot, we both stopped and looked back. My skin continued to crawl with paranoia.

"He's not the one responsible," Thane said, his eyes narrowed at the building. "But I'd be willing to bet my wings he knows who is."

Invisible eyes followed us as we got back into my car and drove away.

CHAPTER 12

Sunday Evening

Thane walked back into the conference room carrying a bag of takeout from *La Carreta*. We had spent the majority of the afternoon and evening going through the three victim's files, researching any similarities, and even pulling up other missing persons reports. Nothing. We hadn't gotten a single lead, nothing that would help us identify the necromancer responsible. He or she was a ghost in the Community.

Not literally, I hoped. I was fairly certain ghosts couldn't do much of anything except scare people.

Thane set the plastic bag down in front of me, careful to avoid a stack of papers. The smells drifting out of the bag made my stomach clench with long-forgotten hunger. "You need to eat."

He certainly didn't need to tell me twice. I dove into the contents without delay, nearly groaning in delight when the onion and garlic of the chicken hit my tastebuds. How the hell did he know *arroz con pollo* was a favorite of mine? Chances were it had been an easy guess since it was a simple yet classic Cuban meal. The real question was who *didn't* love it?

"You didn't get anything for yourself?" I asked around a mouthful of chicken and rice.

Thane smirked as he took his seat across from me and opened his laptop. "Reapers don't eat."

"Yeah, but don't you, like, want to? This smell must be torture." I shoveled another forkful in.

"It does smell divine and makes me miss my mother's cooking, and Cuban food in general, but I can't."

"Can't or won't?"

"It's the same type of thing that keeps humans from noticing reapers when we're working," he explained. "If I even tried to eat, my hand would find something else to do."

"How sad. But you keep coffee in your apartment," I pointed out after taking a quick breather from my food and a sip of water. "Well, you keep something that passes itself off as coffee, anyway."

He groaned and shook his head with a sheepish smile. "My mom brought that blend. It's definitely not what I would choose."

"No?"

"I preferred the smooth, rich flavor of espresso." He sorted through the papers on the conference table, which meant he missed my raised eyebrows. I had no idea he liked real coffee considering what I had found in his apartment. As a coffee aficionado and snob, my respect for the reaper slid up a notch. My love for coffee was the only reason I still kept my day job, provided my boss Isaac hadn't fired me without telling me.

"Okay, so what do we know so far?" I asked, lifting another forkful of chicken to my mouth.

"Not much more than we did before this activity." Thane sighed and leaned back in the chair, his gaze moving from the computer to various piles of papers, a chaotic mess that was mildly organized in his brain. Also a file clerk's worst nightmare.

"There's no connection between the victims," he continued, "The female didn't Rise but had the markings, probably his first attempt. Then there was the first man who did Rise but lost his connection to the mage before we got to him. And last is the shifter you found. No family relations, no genetic relations, no similar hobbies. They didn't live in the same neighborhoods, they didn't work in the same fields, nada." He steepled his fingers in front of his face.

"So the only connection is the lack of one. Totally random." I chewed as I thought.

"Right, which might mean he's trying to cover his tracks." Thane shuffled through the papers until he uncovered a worn book. After flipping through the yellowing pages to a place marked with a scrap of paper, he pushed it toward me. "This contains a lot of useful information on the symbols and the bond to the mage."

I glanced at the text warily while chewing. The author had handwritten the text as small as possible while still being legible, cramming as many words onto the pages as possible. I swallowed my food. "Can you give me the tl;dr version?"

"The what?" Thane blinked at me, looking so dumbfounded that I almost laughed.

"Too long, didn't read. There's no way I'm reading all this." What I didn't want to admit was that my mild dyslexia was going to have a field day trying to read that tiny text. I liked an over-sized font on a screen typically reserved for people with grey hair and reading glasses.

"Just review the third paragraph." He returned to skimming pages in another book.

Holding back a groan, I shoveled another forkful of chicken into my mouth and did as told.

Each symbol must be carved with expert precision to allow for the Rising. Any inconsistencies will cause a failed attempt at worse, a short Rising if lucky, or an untethered bond if unlucky. An untethered can still be herded in a group and, under the proper handling of a well-trained mage, controlled by magic. The downside to this method is proximity. The mage(s) controlling the untethered must remain close enough to maintain the spell.

I blinked when I finished the paragraph without too much trouble. I guess my teachers were right when they said liking a subject would help me focus on the words. Too bad I couldn't study necromancy in school.

"The Risen in the morgue, do we know if they were untethered?" I asked.

Thane scanned another page as he answered, "The first two were, but the one you found was a true success."

"What do you think he's doing that made the shifter talk? Or was it simply because the guy was a shifter before becoming a Risen?"

Thane stopped reviewing his book to pick up the shifter's photo, studying it beneath furrowed brows. "I wish I knew, but this is new territory for us. No record exists of a Community member being turned into a Risen before. As far as I know, it shouldn't be possible."

When I finished the last of my takeout, I pushed the container back and slumped in my chair with a groan, my hands across my stomach. "I'm going to have to call it a night. I can't think on a full belly, and now I have to hit the gym tomorrow before my…" I glanced at him, not wanting to mention Colin yet, "my afternoon shift at the coffee shop."

Thane smirked. "You mean your date?"

I frowned. "How did you know?"

"You weren't exactly whispering on the phone." He raised a knowing eyebrow. "Why don't you want to mention it?"

I let out an exasperated sigh as I stood. "Because I don't know if anything is even going to come of it. This would be our second date, and the first, he ran out on me, right in the middle of it." I gathered up the takeout and tossed it in the trash.

"He ran out? On you?" He actually looked surprised, making the butterflies do a little dance in my overly full stomach. It was not a good feeling.

"Like he suddenly remembered something he had to do," I said. "Anyway, he said he needed to meet with—"

The blaring tones of an alarm cut me off, followed by red and white flashing lights in every direction. Thane snapped his gaze toward the door as it opened and another reaper stuck his head in. "We need all agents down in the lobby now."

"What's the threat?" Thane stood, nearly knocking over his chair in the process.

"Risen. A ton of them," the other reaper said before ducking back out.

Holy shit. That had escalated quickly. Two successes and now this guy was sending a ton? Just how many was that? And why was he sending them here? I followed Thane at a run to the emergency stairwell and down two flights of steps to the DEA's lobby. We exited the stairs and entered into absolute chaos.

The floor-to-ceiling windows that made up the entire entry wall and lobby doors were splattered with blood and sticky guts. A few Risen that were little more than torsos continued to crawl toward their desired meals using just their arms, or in one case just teeth, the arms nowhere to be seen. The sharp tang of copper mixed with garbage left out in the summer sun hit my nose hard and made my eyes water.

A ton turned out to be a very literal estimate. There were far too many to count—the random body parts still moving didn't make it any easier—and it was difficult to know which were actually dead-dead now and not the reanimated dead. The reapers fought off the groaning Risen with deadly accuracy using their scythes and hands, and it became clear they were trying not to kill them all despite the carnage. They needed at least one alive and still tethered to its maker.

Thane grabbed the closest Risen and did his weird reaper sleeper hold on him—one hand around its forehead and one around the back of its neck. The body collapsed into his arms. Thane shouted to another reaper to help him get that one to the lab before the bond to its master could be severed, if it wasn't already.

Unlike traditional human stories of zombies, only a necromantic mage could make other Risen. As far as I knew, a bite would just hurt or get infected or get you killed if you couldn't get yourself loose and they ate the rest of you. Facing a Risen wasn't anywhere close to the biggest threat to the Community, but en masse was a whole other story.

I stayed back and leaned against a wall, knowing the reapers had it under control despite the chaos. Besides, I didn't want to get blood all over myself. I wasn't being a prude, but going more than a week without having to dry clean my clothes would be nice. I could only come up with so many excuses for the cleaners who gave me weird looks lately.

One of the Risen ambled toward me with his arms outstretched, rotting flesh drooping toward the foyer floor. I let out a sigh, resigning myself to the idea of needing to fight. Before I could draw a blade, a line appeared on the Risen's neck, and his head slid off his body with a disgusting slurp. The rest of the body crumpled, revealing a reaper in a dress and high heels wielding her metal scythe. She winked at me before moving on to the next.

What a badass.

When the fight was over and all the Risen captured or truly dead via decapitation or a blade in the brain, Thane joined me. Crimson and black splattered across his pants and shirt. He ran a hand through his hair, careful to use his dry one. Sadly, it wouldn't have mattered—a chunk of something that looked an awful lot like skin nestled in his dark strands.

"I've got to help clean up and find out if any are still tethered," he said. "Are you flying or driving back to your place?"

"Driving." If I flew, I'd have to eat again and the thought of doing that after the Cuban takeout and witnessing the blood fest in front of me made my stomach churn. Making it home without puking once would be a miracle.

"Let me walk you to the garage," he said.

"Oh please, I'm not some helpless damsel in distress." I put a hand up to stop his protest and tucked my other hand under my nose. "Also, you stink like rotten guts, and I don't want to lose my dinner all over your shoes."

I was completely telling the truth, too. In addition to whatever was stuck to his hair, one of the bodies had left parts of itself behind on his shirt cuff and sleeve, a fact I was trying really hard not to notice.

"Fine, but don't try to be a hero if more show up," he said, his gaze already refocused on cleanup activities. "There's an alarm button on every floor."

"Aye aye, captain." I saluted him and headed back down the stairwell to the garage.

It was quiet, eerily so, but I attributed my heightened nerves to the attack upstairs. My footsteps echoing off the concrete walls were the only sound as I approached my car, but a shiver slithered up my spine and shook my shoulders. I turned to look behind and around me, using my enhanced vision to pick up any heat signatures. Nothing. Not a peep, not even from the crickets.

And yet my skin continued to crawl as I slid into my car and locked the doors. I double checked the back seats, which were as empty as they should have been. I opened the glove box and pulled out my gun, laying it on my lap. With one hand on the weapon, I backed out of the parking spot with the other. Better to be prepared for action.

Still, nothing changed as I approached the exit ramp and chanced one final glance in my rearview mirror. Glowing yellow eyes in a shadowy recess of the garage stared back at me, unmistakable in the dark. Not one to back away from a threat, I stomped on my brakes, threw the car into park, and got out, my heart pounding as I raised my gun.

The eyes were gone and the garage was empty, leaving me with nothing but a creeping sense of foreboding.

CHAPTER 13

Monday Morning

I hadn't heard from my boss yet on whether or not I was welcome back at the coffee shop, so I assumed I wouldn't be working my Monday afternoon shift. If Isaac thought I was kidding when I said to let me know when I was welcome back, then he clearly didn't know me very well after three years.

Today was the day Xavier would be beheaded, so I would have called in sick anyway. Nothing in this world would stop me from being there to watch his head roll.

I worked off some frustration and paranoia from last night's events by lifting weights at my local gym. Because I was certain my imagination got the best of me after the Risen attack, I decided not to mention the glowing eyes in the garage to anyone, not even Kit. The last thing I needed was even more watchful eyes on me by way of Jessa or another lurking angel.

After the workout, I got ready for my date with Colin. It would be a casual lunch, and I didn't want to seem too eager to please, so I chose a pair of white linen shorts and sandals that complimented my tanned legs. Add in a pale pink off-the-shoulder blouse that would lighten the purple color of my eyes to a lilac, a few swipes of mascara, a couple curls of my blonde hair, and I was out the door.

Colin beat me to the little French cafe downtown even though I got there a few minutes early, a fact I liked quite a bit. A blue-and-white striped awning hung overhead to keep the blazing sun from spoiling the ambiance. The fae stood as I approached on the outdoor patio and pulled out a white wicker chair for me. Like the first day we met, he wore an untucked polo in pale yellow and slim cut jeans that showed off his shapely derrière. When in France…or just a French cafe.

"What a gentleman." I took the offered seat. "Is this part of your apology?"

"Ah, I'm afraid not." He sat in his chair again and grinned. "Just part of my natural charm."

In the daylight, his hair displayed those beautiful streaks of red that made it more of a light auburn. The greenery of the hanging plants and palm trees around us enhanced the green of his eyes, though the blue showed up every time he smiled. Fae eyes in all their glory. As before, the rest of his features were glamoured to appear human.

"But now that it's been brought up," he continued, "I

do want to sincerely apologize for my atrocious behavior." He reached across the table and took my hand, his gaze holding mine as he attempted a sad puppy face. "Will you ever be able to forgive me?"

My heart did a little pitter-patter, and I pursed my lips as I tried not to laugh. He was so unlike any of the other fae I'd heard stories about, I almost wouldn't have believed he was one if I didn't know Joe already. Usually their kind took brooding and dangerous to a whole new level.

"I think I can be persuaded to forgive you," I said. "Just don't let it happen again."

"Never." He winked as he sat back. "I'm sure you've heard by now that there was an attack on the DEA last night."

"I was there."

He blinked at me, startled. "What?"

"I'm working with one of the agents on the case. Unofficially."

"That makes two of us." He chuckled, though he still seemed slightly caught off guard. "You weren't hurt, were you?"

"No, I stayed out of the attack and let the reapers do their thing." I shooed a fly away from my face—the downside to eating outside in a city competing with the sun's heat. "Plus, I didn't want to have to dry clean my clothes."

"Sound reason," he said with a grin. "I had to leave from our first date so abruptly to discuss the Risen you found with Adam. I guess we'll have a lot in common to talk about now."

I made a face. "I'm not sure discussing dead people is ideal for getting to know each other, but I'll take it."

He laughed. "No, I suppose you're right."

After we ordered food—the perfect pairing of a rich, buttery croissant and a black coffee for me and a hearty plate of eggs and iced tea for him—the topics turned to more light-hearted ones like music and travel. I marveled at how easy it was to talk to Colin, and I felt like I had known him for months or years rather than just a few days. He may not have set my skin aflame with his touch, but he was very much alive. Vibrant and enticing.

Besides, nothing good ever came from getting too close to a fire. For most people, anyway, but I clung to the original thought. My phone buzzed at some point, but I ignored it. Tried to, anyway. After the fifth buzz, I picked it up.

"Sorry, let me just check who's..." My voice trailed off as I read the message and my heart stuttered to a stop. The world drifted away as my blood froze, and pinpricks appeared in my vision until I remembered to take a shuddering breath.

Colin's voice released the vise-like hold on my heart. "What happened?"

"Xavier," I whispered, as if the Master Vampire would hear his name on my lips. "He escaped."

"How is that possible?"

"I don't know." My hands shook as I responded with a quick note to Thane who had asked if I was safe. I set the phone down next to my plate and stared at it.

For the most part over the last two days, I had been able to stop thinking about the vampire's beheading. Everything going on with the Risen, Thane, and even Colin had completely taken over valuable real estate in my brain, and it had been almost a relief to set the sadistic vampire out of my thoughts for the weekend.

But now those thoughts and feelings returned with a vengeance. The Risen attack and the Master Vampire's escape from the DEA building had to be connected. There was zero percent chance that those two events were purely coincidental. But vampires and necromancers didn't usually help each other out. Creating the Risen took away from a vampire's food source, after all. So why would someone go to the trouble to help Xavier?

And even more importantly in my book, would he be coming after me next?

Colin reached across the table to grip my now-clammy hand again. "You're safe. He won't come after you."

His grip was smooth yet firm, and I focused on his nearness to stop my racing thoughts. I attempted a smile as he seemed to read my mind. "I appreciate the reassurance, but we don't really know that."

"He's a smart man." He squeezed my hand reassuringly. "He'll know you're being protected now that he's out."

Colin might be right, but that didn't mean I wouldn't take every precaution to keep myself safe. If the Master Vampire did show his face, I would be more than prepared to send him back to the grave for good, or die trying. More than anything else, the prospect of getting to be the one to kill him raised my spirits.

"Didn't you say you were working with one of the reapers?" Colin asked. "Surely he or she will be keeping watch on you."

I rolled my eyes, more fear doused with mention of the reaper. "I doubt that. Thane Munro isn't exactly the type to think of others above himself."

"Thane…I know the name, if not the face."

"Tall, dark, and brooding. You can't really miss him," I said without thinking.

Colin chuckled. "Sounds like competition."

I made a face, although I could feel my body responding in a different way to the mere mention of the reaper. "Let's not forget the fact that he's dead."

I might have been reminding myself of that fact more than Colin.

"Well, I can certainly say I've got him beat on that front," he said and lifted his glass in a toast.

I laughed and raised my glass to clink against his. "You most definitely do."

After lunch and a promise to schedule another date soon, I headed for *el Mercado Sombra* where I agreed to meet with my client Tabitha again. With its mysterious magic not allowing any violence within its confines, the market would be one of the safest, if not *the* safest, place for a meeting now that Xavier was on the loose. Clearly the DEA wasn't even as secure a spot anymore.

I had sent Tabitha a message explaining what Luka said about getting the ring when she returned to the pack, and she had requested to see me in person. My hands were tied, but I didn't want to be rude, so I agreed. I felt for the woman, and I had promised to get the ring back for her. But pack politics and dominance had me at a standstill.

Unless I were to steal—

Nope. Those days were done. Being falsely charged with a murder and soul-theft was enough to convince me of the error of my ways. Or at least that I enjoyed having my pretty little head attached to my body more than I enjoyed the thrill of the hunt, but just barely.

Once again, I found an empty picnic table near the food carts and stalls, more easily this time since it was after the lunch crowd, and waited. She was almost ten minutes late today and arrived in a breathless rush. Her thick brown hair was pulled up into a messy bun, and she had on a stained, once-white apron over a wrinkled restaurant uniform.

"I'm sorry to keep you waiting," Tabitha panted. "Work ran over. Thank you for not leaving."

"No worries at all," I said.

Her honey-brown eyes opened wide and a hand flew to her mouth. "Oh gosh! Thank you for coming at all. I heard about the Master Vampire's escape."

"What better place to be than the market?" I smiled, though I had to fake it a bit. Xavier was once again infiltrating my thoughts instead of being dead. "I'm the one who should be sorry. My hands are tied with this case, but Luka might be more understanding and willing if the request came from you."

She sat down across from me and blew loose strands of hair out of her face. "You don't understand. I can't go back there."

"Because he killed your father?" It was a total guess, but I had a fifty percent chance of being right.

Her face paled. "He told you?"

"Only that your father was the last alpha. I filled in the gaps."

"I *loved* Luka." Her voice was bitter, and her grip tightened on her purse. "We were to be married, but then he challenged my father for supremacy. I will never forgive him for that."

Despite her words, regret flashed across her features. I would be willing to bet a hefty sum that she still loved the wolf and wanted to forgive him. Why did pride always get in the way of these things?

"I understand," I said, "but maybe if you go to him as a widow—"

"I don't want the ring for sentimental reasons," she interrupted.

I blinked at her. "I'm not sure why that matters."

"The ring has been imbued with magic to protect the wearer," she explained. "It's given to the beta to ensure the next strongest will survive if the alpha falls."

Made sense, just not why she wanted it this bad.

"Children of werewolves do not become werewolves unless they're infected with the virus. It's typically done in a ceremony just after puberty." Tabitha glanced around to make sure no one was close enough to listen, as I was fairly certain she was revealing some pack secrets. I leaned forward, eager to learn more. "The alpha infects the next generation of wolves with a bite, but someone wearing the ring will be protected even from that. The metal has been enchanted so that the wearer hardly notices it and won't take it off."

I gazed into her eyes, identifying the fear she tried to keep in check. "You want the ring for your son."

She closed her eyes for a moment, and a tear squeezed out. "Yes. I want it to be his choice whether or not he joins the pack, when he's old enough to understand the full consequences of his decision."

I furrowed my eyebrows. "I thought it already was."

"Only if you consider being brainwashed a choice." Her short laugh held no humor. "I left the pack because they would fill his head with nothing but the glory and excitement of being a wolf until it became the only option in his mind, just like it'd been for me. There's much more to the decision, and most of it's far from glorious. Luka knows that, but the pack always comes first." Her last words were saturated with bitterness and a hint of longing.

I leaned my chin onto the palm of my hand, elbow resting on the picnic table. Now that she left the pack, Luka would never give her the ring willingly. As the daughter of the previous alpha and widow of the last beta, it was Tabitha's sacred duty within the pack to choose the next beta if the alpha didn't choose her as his mate. The man I had met outside the house, the wolf currently in the role of beta, might not be her choice if she returned.

No wonder the man had looked at me with such contempt. Or maybe even fear.

Luka had to know why she wanted the ring, and I had a feeling he would give it to her if it were his choice alone. But as alpha, he had his wolves to protect first and foremost. And if Tabitha didn't return to the pack, then she and her son weren't his concern.

But I kept coming around to the fact that Luka was still in love with Tabitha. I rubbed my lip with a finger. If he loved her as much as his eyes told me he did, then he just might be willing to look the other way while I snuck in and relieved him of the ring. Or maybe he wouldn't even notice it was missing. A wishful thought.

Stealing the ring would make me the wolves' next target—if they caught me. I would have to cover up my scent, avoid any bloodshed, and get in and out as fast as possible. No need to involve Kit as this would be a pretty basic job and she would likely disapprove and talk me out of it.

Fuck. I had just made up my mind. I met Tabitha's hopeful gaze. She knew.

CHAPTER 14

Monday Afternoon

Once again, Thane was meeting me at Kit's place to keep his involvement with my brother's case to a minimum. I left Tabitha with a promise but also made sure she understood it could take me a few days, if not longer, to attempt stealing personal goods from the resident werewolf alpha. I tried very hard to ignore the tingles of anticipation spreading through my limbs when I thought about that job.

The abundance of Risen suddenly showing up was the main obstacle for not completing the job sooner. If I brought Kit into the job, the research part of the gig would go significantly faster, but maybe it was time for me to learn some new tricks in that department. Not that I would ever want to part ways with Kit, but who knew what the future held.

From my place on Kit's couch—a new piece after the manticore incident left holes too big to fix in the last one—I did my best not to stare at Thane's face while he made pleasantries with my best friend. She wasn't big into idle chit chat, but even she wouldn't ignore basic etiquette by discussing the weather with a guest in her home.

The reaper's features drew my gaze to him like a signal fire. I wanted to trace the lines of his chiseled jaw with my fingers or even my tongue, run my hands through his lusciously thick hair to see if it felt as velvety as it looked, and press my lips against his, knowing already how full and soft they were. I wondered if Thane and I would ever get a chance to be alone again and just see where that heat took us.

Ugh. I rubbed my face, trying to banish that line of thinking. I didn't even know why I still cared to know how hot the reaper's touch would get, not with Colin in my life. Thinking of the fae and our easy conversations brought a smile to my face. He might not have set my skin on fire with his mere touch, but he was about as good as anyone could get with the added bonus of being alive and capable of giving me babies. The fact that I even considered someone's dead-or-alive state spoke volumes about how low my desperation had sunk.

I sighed.

"You okay, girl?" Kit asked, turning her attention on me and away from the small talk—making me into a fantastic decoy to escape.

I shook myself, needing to stay in the moment and not get lost in fantasy worlds that would never happen. I faked a yawn. "Yeah, just tired."

Thane frowned. "Not so tired that you were followed, I hope. You need to keep your wits about you now that Xavier is out. His ability to hold grudges for centuries is legendary."

I ground my teeth. I wasn't really tired, it was just the first thing that popped out of my mouth. Of course I was being careful. Ridiculously paranoid, even, especially now that I was plotting to steal from an alpha werewolf. I knew there was a hypocritical moment in that line of thinking, but I decided not to focus on it. I still had time to change my mind on the whole werewolf thing if I needed to, after all.

"My wits are perfectly about, thank you very much," I said, more snappily than I intended. "How did Xavier escape, anyway? Why was he even still at HQ and not at the prison?"

The jail at the DEA headquarters was meant to be a temporary holding facility, much like any human police station. Community prisoners would be held there immediately before and after trials, and before being released or moved to their new cell block digs. In my not-so-humble opinion, he should have been immediately returned to the maximum-security Community prison once the sentencing wrapped up. Too bad no one asked me what I thought.

"It should have been safer to keep him there than risk transporting him twice before his execution." Thane sighed. "I have a feeling it wouldn't have mattered either way."

"So, is he a necromancer now?" I asked. "Is that even possible in his undead state?"

"No, vampires can't harness magic, but he obviously has some sort of connection. We just haven't figured out who or why yet." He approached me with the file he carried, and Kit disappeared into her bedroom.

My heartbeat immediately started to race as I eyed the folder. A sense of déjà vu invaded my thoughts, only it was real—we had been here, done this before.

"Do you want me to stay?" Thane asked, his voice soft and kind. I might even go so far as to say caring. A tone I hadn't quite expected to ever hear coming from him.

My heart warmed and relaxed at the sound, and I nodded and swallowed the lump in my throat. I was about to find out everything about Maddox's real death. "I may have questions."

While that was true, I also felt calm in his presence when I wasn't thinking about how good he would be in bed. The heat he gave off soothed my frazzled nerves.

He took a seat near me on the couch, close but not directly beside me, giving me space while also providing comfort should I need it. Warmth spread over me like a welcome blanket as it drifted off him.

I took the folder and opened it, this time more prepared to see Maddox's beautiful smile. It still hurt, but far less than the first time. I ran my finger over the lines of his face before moving on. Along with his detailed personal information, the file included some basic facts about our parents, Rhiannon and Drystan Neill, and their move into the Miami area twenty-six years ago, a year after I was born. No mention was made of where they had moved from, a question they always avoided when I asked, but that was a mystery for another day.

It shouldn't have surprised me the agency had so much information on our little family, and yet it still did. I skimmed through the details I already knew, not wanting to get bogged down by my memories as they threatened to swell to the surface. I stopped when I found something new. The man responsible for Mad's murder was being held at the Community prison outside of Fort Myers—the same one Xavier would have been in prior to his sentencing.

This man had been only a couple hundred miles away the whole time. My breath caught in my throat.

There was no reason provided for why he did what he did, but the evidence piled up against him, including the purchase of items for use in illegal magical practices. He had used magic to sneak in and out of our house, but he didn't make any attempt to cover up his tracks prior to that. It was almost like he wanted to be caught.

But then why cover up the murder to look like a suicide? And why the fuck did the agency keep this a secret from me?

"Why did he do it?" I asked, my voice little more than a whisper.

"I don't know," Thane said. I hadn't really expected a response, but it was nice of him to provide one.

"I want to go see him," I said, gripping the sides of the folder hard enough to dent the stiff paper.

"They don't allow visitors. I already checked into it."

"Not even for me?" I asked, looking up. There must be a loophole somewhere. "His victim's only surviving family?"

"Especially not for you, I'm afraid."

I glared at him and slammed the file closed. "Then I'll break in. Kit will help me."

"Yeah, no," her voice chimed in from her open

bedroom door. "It's one thing to hack into a less-protected facility like the DEA headquarters, and a whole other ballgame to break into a maximum-security prison while there's a necromancer wreaking havoc. I'd find my ass thrown inside so fast."

"Ask Adam," I said to Thane, desperation clinging to my words. The Archangel of Miami was the reaper's boss. If he agreed, pretty much anything could happen.

"I did." His eyes were soft despite the sternness in his face. He wanted to help me, I could tell, but I was too angry and full of emotions to care.

"Obviously not very hard," I snapped. "I'll ask him myself."

Thane narrowed his eyes, the softness fleeing. "Be my guest."

Shit. I had offended him. I hadn't meant to, but damn, it was really hard to control my mouth sometimes, especially when it came to the reaper. First, he brought me a horribly redacted file, and now I knew the man who did it was imprisoned but not why he did it in the first place or anything more about him. Getting bits and pieces here and there was grating on my last few nerves. I squeezed the bridge of my nose in response to the rising throb in my head.

"I'll let you read over the rest." After standing and taking his teleportation device out of his pocket, Thane pushed the button to activate the portal. The black circle appeared on the floor, ready to whisk him away. "Let me know if you have any other questions."

Before I could even open my mouth to apologize, he was gone.

"Fuck." I slumped into the couch cushions.

"You really need to be nicer to that guy," Kit said as she walked back into the living room.

"I can't help it. He's so goddamn smug sometimes."

"That makes two of you." Kit headed for the door, looking rather pretty with a hint of mascara, a light blue floral top that showed off her variety of tattoos, and cute yellow shorts. The colors popped fantastically against her dark complexion. She had even pulled her braids up into an elaborate bun. All in all, an outfit very unlike Kit. I hadn't taken a good look at her before.

"Did you get a job I don't know about?" I turned around on the couch to watch her, leaning my chin on my forearm.

She snorted. "Unlike you, I don't need to have a cover job. I work in cyber security. That usually shuts people up."

"So where ya headed?"

"Date." She reached for her bag by the door and slung it over her shoulder.

She must really want to make a good impression with that look. "Who's the lucky gal?"

Her cheeks turned the slightest shade of pink. Kit blushing. Holy shit. The world was coming to an end.

"Her name is Angela," she said, as if that would be enough.

Did she even know me? "And…?"

"And what?" Kit tucked her phone into the purse.

I sighed. "What is she? Another witch? Fae?"

She avoided my gaze. "She's a…witch."

"Why do you say it like that?"

"She's a human witch."

My heart sank. "Oh. Are you sure this is such a good idea? I can't help but notice you're going out of your way to make an impression."

"Are you sure it's a good idea to fall for a reaper?" she countered, leveling her dark brown eyes on mine.

"I'm not... what makes you... why..." I sputtered.

"Oh, please, Veronica, you're not fooling anyone," she said, unlocking the deadbolt and grabbing the handle. "But don't judge me for my messy bed when yours is no better."

"I'm not judging you, I'm worried about that big softy heart of yours."

"I'm a grown ass woman." Her expression softened, but she didn't take her hand off the door. "Sometimes it pays to be vulnerable, sometimes it doesn't. But you'll never know if you never try. Love you."

"You, too. Have fun." I smooched the air in her direction as she left. Leave it to the nearly-one-hundred-year-old witch to part with such sage advice. And the bitch didn't even look thirty yet.

Then I was alone. Alone with a file telling me that my brother had been murdered by a member of the Community, and said person was being held in a prison so close and yet still so far—I wasn't even allowed to go in and ask questions. It didn't matter how many miles away it was if I couldn't get access to face this guy.

Thane might have tried to convince Adam on my behalf, but Adam hadn't said no to me directly yet, and I could be very persuasive. Time to see an angel, and maybe even bribe him.

What would it take to sway an angel—an *archangel*?

CHAPTER 15

Monday Evening

I hadn't been to the DEA headquarters for an actual meeting before, so I hoped I could just show up without an appointment. A little arrogant, perhaps—okay, maybe a lot arrogant—but then I *was* the last phoenix asking for an audience with the local archangel. If I couldn't get in whenever I wanted, I didn't know anyone who could. Worst case scenario would be my ass thrown out on the street. I could handle that.

Much like Xavier had overseen all vampiric activities in the area as Miami's previous Master Vampire, Adam reigned over all the other angels in south Florida as the archangel. Oh, and also over all the Community members as well, including the vampires. He was the resident VIP, and I wasn't sure if higher levels of angels really existed or if the rumor was there to encourage people to behave. There might have been a grand total of two sightings of virtues (the next level up in the angelic choir) in the last few hundred centuries, but the accounts were shaky at best. Not quite trustworthy.

Since Kit knew significantly more about the Community species, I once asked her if Adam was *the* Adam, as in the original man who became an angel. I was slightly disappointed to learn he wasn't; his name was just the most popular of his time thousands of years ago.

A few reapers glanced at me with raised eyebrows in the elevator on my way up, noting that the button for the tenth floor, the top floor and their boss's level, was lit. I gave them a courteous nod and continued twiddling my thumbs behind my back.

When the door dinged and opened on its last stop, I was alone, all the reapers having come and gone. The archangel didn't appear to get many visitors, or perhaps they knew he wasn't here. Or maybe he expected visitors to set up appointments. I stepped into the foyer.

The room was longer and narrower than I expected, considering Adam's office was supposed to be the only thing up here. A tan leather couch sat along the wall to my right and a few matching chairs faced each other on the left. Both seating areas were complete with glass-top coffee tables, holding an array of magazines from the last several decades. Besides the furniture, a few potted trees, and the receptionist's desk, the room was barren.

"The Archangel is busy at the moment," the reaper receptionist said after I requested an audience with his semi-holiness. Her dark blonde hair was pulled up into a sleek, perfectionist bun that made me think she might have been a ballerina in her previous life. The idea suited the elegant lines of her bone structure and poise. "He does have some time tomorrow afternoon."

"I'll wait until he's not busy" I started to turn for the couch in the foyer.

"Honey, you could be waiting all night," she said, raising an eyebrow over her tortoiseshell glasses.

I shrugged. "That just means I won't be late for our meeting tomorrow."

She clucked her tongue but didn't stop me from settling in.

The three-seater couch was actually quite comfortable and even had a decorative pillow I could use for my head if it came to it. I might have been displaying my overly stubborn side with this move, but I wouldn't fail my brother again. I needed to face his murderer and find out why he did it.

I contented myself with the few magazines lying about, mostly of human happenings and politics, but interesting enough for now. I must have dozed off at some point, though, because the next time I opened my eyes, Adam's face peered down at mine.

"You're quite persistent," he said, a hint of amusement crossing his features. He wore his sand-colored hair closely cropped to his head, which only made the chiseled line of his jaw stand out more. I guessed that was his goal. He was built like a linebacker, lean muscle for speed but still tough as a brick wall. Not the kind of man you crossed.

I stumbled to my feet. "Persistent is a huge understatement."

He turned away, his blindingly white wings tucked snugly against his back. With the feathers out of the way, the outer edges of his wings just barely brushed the door into his office. Since the building was of modern human construction, the doorframe was wider than average for disability accommodations, but it also turned out handy for angels. He left it open after he entered, a sign I took to mean I was welcome to follow. The receptionist winked at me as I passed, and I grinned back.

Inside, I closed the door behind me and approached the angel. Mahogany bookshelves lined the entire right wall, filled to the brim with massive leather tomes with gilded lettering and crumbling, yellowing manuscripts. I was sure some people like Kit would drool over the sight of all those ancient books, but to me it was just a collection of more old, dead things, waiting to trip up my dyslexia. Rude.

The left wall was all glass, with a sliding door opening onto an empty balcony or terrace. At night, it was impossible to tell how large the outside area was since all I saw was the reflection of the room. I assumed the balcony was used primarily for flight, or, if he was like me, a little help thinking through problems while he gazed out over the ocean. I liked the idea of us being similar—it meant he was more likely to help me.

A massive wooden desk, the same rich mahogany as the shelves, took up the majority of the rest of the room, with two matching chairs for visitors facing it. Behind his desk hung a behemoth of a painting in a gilded ornamental frame.

The portrait was of a young man with long brown hair and a lovely smile. I could only assume this was Jesus of Nazareth, just not the typical Christ on a cross portrait I saw everywhere else and expected here. The smile was a nice change, reminding visitors of the man who lived rather than the man who died.

My gaze drifted back to the angel. Had he known Jesus in person?

Adam gestured to one of the chairs at his desk as he moved to sit at his. The wide back of his chair had been replaced with a thin one, allowing it to sneak up his back and between his wings. As he relaxed, his wings spread naturally to each side, the brilliant white catching the light so that the feathers appeared to shimmer.

"To what do I owe the pleasure of your late-night visit, Ms. Neill?"

"V is fine," I said as I sat across from him. "I'd like to visit my brother's murderer."

The angel steepled his fingers in front of his face, his elbows resting on the chair's arms. "What do you hope to accomplish?"

"I need to know why he did it, why he killed a sixteen-year-old boy." My voice broke slightly on the last word, but I didn't break Adam's blue gaze.

"Is it not enough to know your brother did not die by his own hand, and the man responsible is serving his time?"

I shook my head. "I need a reason. This wasn't some random act of killing. It was planned, and he knew he would be caught."

Adam regarded me for a few silent moments. "I see. I am sorry to be the bearer of bad news, but visitors are not permitted."

"Why?"

Adam raised his eyebrows, probably at my boldness to question an angel. I wasn't too worried about any real repercussions, though. He might never have been anything other than an angel, but he understood the rest of us and our impulses. It was part of his job.

"It is punishment for the convict and safety precautions for everyone else."

"Surely you can override that," I said.

"Surely I can," he said. "But I will not."

I sighed. "I don't understand. Why even let me see the file?"

"I had hoped your curiosity would be satisfied."

"You don't know me very well."

He smiled. "Clearly."

We sat in silence for a few moments while I tried to think of another way to get him to approve. Nothing came to mind and I was mentally and emotionally exhausted. I was also fairly sure I could still convince Kit to help me get into the prison.

"Okay, well, thank you for your time," I said as I stood. "Don't be surprised if I ask Colin to come bug you next."

The angel tilted his head to the side. "Who?"

Oh, shit. Maybe I was being too informal. I didn't really know anything about their meetings. "Colin Ó Broin."

Adam shook his head. "I'm afraid I don't know him."

I blinked at him. "Fae guy with auburn hair and beautiful blue-green eyes? Meets with you about the Risen issue on behalf of the prince?"

"I do not discuss the situation with anyone outside the agency," the archangel said, his face darkening. "I suspect you are being fooled."

My mouth dropped open. Why the hell would Colin lie to me? Or was Adam simply trying to cover up the fae's involvement? One of them was lying to me or fudging the truth. Fae weren't capable of lying, but they were masters of twisting words to form a new truth. And angels most definitely could and did lie when they needed to.

Fuck. Had I just gotten Colin in trouble?

CHAPTER 16

Monday Night

Things had gotten confusing again. I left Adam shortly after he said he didn't know Colin. Either the archangel was lying to me or Colin was twisting the truth, and I hated being played a fool more than I hated Xavier. Okay, maybe not quite as much as that. I seethed every time I thought of the bloodsucker while I could be known to go soft for a beautiful man batting his eyelashes at me in apology.

But it was a close second.

I didn't have to work at the coffee shop super early in the morning—if I even still worked there, Isaac hadn't messaged yet to ask why I had missed my afternoon shift—

so I decided to take an evening stroll home by way of downtown Miami while I mulled over my predicament. I wasn't being stupid or careless; my penthouse was only a few blocks away. The streets were also far too busy for a vampire to approach me in public, especially a Master Vampire on the run. I was sure Adam had someone keeping a closer eye on me, too, a fact which Xavier would consider.

And hey, maybe I would get the chance to kill him and work out some of my pent-up anger. Maybe I was kind of hoping he'd come out to play. I wasn't wholly unprepared for an encounter. As soon as I made the decision to visit Adam, I added a few stakes to the normal arsenal hidden beneath my clothes.

I drifted down the mostly quiet Monday night streets— quiet for Miami, anyway. Cars still rushed by, blaring music from time to time, and restaurants still bustled with the late-evening crowd. The Miami heat wrapped around me like a comforting blanket, soothing me in a way not many things could. Much like one annoying reaper.

I sighed, wishing I hadn't pissed him off. If I hadn't, he might have been willing to snuggle my worries away on my couch. As if snuggling was all we would do.

Refusing to let my mind drift any further in *that* direction, I focused on the here and now. The month of May meant the start of the awful weather season for many, just not for me. With fire in my blood, I loved the heat. Speaking of heat, maybe there would be someone at the prison that I could sweet talk into letting me in. I was sure I could stalk a guard there who was in need of some female companionship.

My jaw clicked as I clenched my teeth. I would stoop to

almost any level to get a chance to face Mad's murderer.

I turned left at the next corner, onto the Brickell Flatiron's street. A familiar bar was just two roads down from there, and my penthouse just another block past that. Grabbing a nightcap at the bar would help settle my nerves, but finishing the trip home with my senses dulled wasn't a super wise idea. Even if it was only one street down.

Before I had time to decide, my heart stopped along with my feet.

Less than a block ahead of me stood Xavier. Not only had he seen me, too, his smile made it clear he tracked me there. Thane must have been right about the vampire's ability to hold grudges.

Talk about careless—only it was *his* carelessness this time.

His hair, normally the rich hues of autumn in the daylight but just a deep brown at night, hung down to curl around his smooth chin. The angles and lines of his face were expertly crafted and, along with his sensuously full lips, designed to draw his prey to him faster than a moth to a flame. As a Master Vampire, his features had had at least a millennium to define themselves like a piece of fine art, part of the allure of becoming a bloodsucker in the first place.

Vampire wannabes just had to be willing to go through a century or two of looking like a B horror film creature first, especially if it took them more than a few days to claw their way out of their coffin and grave.

He sauntered toward me in linen slacks and a floral button-down shirt left open a few buttons at the top, revealing the muscles of his bare chest. I stood my ground and withdrew a stake from my small messenger bag, making no attempt to hide it from his view. His grin grew wider.

"Oh, come now, little bird," he said, "there's no need to fight. You being mine is inevitable."

I laughed. "Me being your final death, maybe."

He tsk-tsked, striding closer. I would need to make a move soon before he expected one. A loose thread drew my gaze to the sleeve of his shirt, where his chiseled bicep peeked out. As his arm moved, thick veins rolled beneath his skin, speaking to the strength of this magnificent creature. He raised a hand to his face to brush his hair behind an ear, and my gaze went right along with the movement. I licked my lips as I eyed him, craving his touch and kiss along every inch of my bod—

I shook my head and glared at him, pushing his invasive thoughts out of my mind. Vampires didn't have the ability to actively control people's minds, but they influenced and enhanced pheromones to draw their prey in. I hated the fact that I found the monster attractive, but resigned myself to knowing that biology meant anyone would. At least I was able to resist his attempts to control me this way.

"No one will be dying here tonight, but you cost me everything, little bird." His eyes narrowed.

"Is that why you're here alone? No friends to help you out?" I taunted, knowing his anger would encourage him to make mistakes.

His upper lip raised in a snarl. "I don't need any help to take back what belongs to me."

"I don't belong to anyone." Now seemed like a good time to strike.

I launched myself toward him, using my inhuman speed and strength to catch him off-guard. That was the hope, anyway. He might have had at least a millennium on me in terms of experience, but he still hadn't come to terms with the fact that women had drastically changed in this world over the last hundred years.

He would underestimate me, and I would use that to my advantage.

With the stake out in front of me, I aimed for his heart. Even as fast as I was going, he managed to smile at me, which pissed me off even further. He turned the stake aside and swooped me into his arms, holding me tightly against him face-to-face.

I let him think he had truly caught me for a moment. His smile turned into a malicious grin, revealing his sharpened, elongated canines. Then I kneed him as hard as I could between his legs.

Priceless.

His grimace of pain and surprise was spectacular. When his arms loosened, I twisted free, coming around behind him. I raised my arm to plunge the stake through his back. I didn't care if it was fighting dirty; he needed to die however I could do it. He was too good, too strong to play fair.

But vampires healed and recovered at atrociously annoying rates, which meant he sidestepped before my stake found skin. He grabbed my wrist and squeezed. I yelped, my bones cracking beneath his grip. I dropped the stake, and he pulled me in close again, a snarl on his lips.

"Fighting against me only gets me more excited to break you," he said, his mouth close enough to smell his raunchy, coppery breath. "They all break in the end."

I glared back at him. "You'd have to catch me first."

Just as I was about to shift to bird form to use my talons

against him, a new voice called out, "Oh, come on, am I going to have to heal you again?"

Xavier spun, not letting go of his grip on my arm even as I grunted in pain, to face the new threat.

Jessa.

My guardian angel's light-pink wings settled against her back as she landed on the sidewalk. Much like the reaper repellant, her angelic cloaking magic would keep any human passersby from noticing our little get-together.

Her long, fire-colored hair, which suited her sprite-like personality, was half pulled up into a mess of curls and ringlets framing her lightly freckled face. Her navy-blue dress slacks hugged her slim curves and tapered at her ankles, and a cream-colored blouse made her hair pop. Not an especially terror-inducing outfit, but her hands on her hips and fierce glare helped.

"Unless you wish to fight *me*," she said, her lagoon-colored eyes narrowing at the vampire, "I suggest you let Veronica go."

"Seriously, Jessa," I said, letting out an exasperated breath, "I had this under control."

Xavier growled but didn't loosen his hold. "One young angel isn't enough to stop a Master Vampire."

"Good thing she's not alone, then," added a voice behind us.

I stumbled and almost fell as Xavier whirled around again. Goddamn blood sucker.

As I righted myself, I glared at an angel I hadn't met before, a man who smiled benevolently at us while holding massive iron chains in his hands. His eyes matched his dark-brown hair, which brushed the top of his broad shoulders, and his wings looked more like Adam's than Jessa's, only with a hint of blue shimmer.

Unlike either of the other mentioned angels, this one only wore a pair of comfortable linen pants. That was it. Bare-footed and bare-chested, the newcomer was almost a head taller than any of us, with muscles for days. If anyone deserved a hearty whistle of appreciation, it was this man. Talk about a guardian angel.

But I wasn't glaring because I was mad at him—I just totally had this situation under control before they arrived. Now they were going to cart Xavier off for a "proper" execution when I wanted to kill him right then and there.

"You're wasting your time coming after me," the vampire hissed. "The true threat has only just begun."

Goosebumps rose along my skin as I shifted my gaze back to Xavier's face. If he didn't consider himself a true threat, what the hell were we about to face?

The new angel raised an eyebrow. "Of what threat do you speak?"

Xavier grinned. "The Risen. You're not dealing with a solitary necromancer."

"No?" Jessa asked, appearing beside me. "How many then? A duo?"

Xavier dropped his grip from my wrist at last and stepped farther away. Despite being the bad guy, even he wouldn't defy an angel straight to her face. At least, I was pretty sure he wouldn't. I held my broken wrist gingerly against my chest with my other hand. Now that I thought about it, he was probably getting ready to run. The new angel must have had the same thought, because his grip tightened on the chains.

"The Society lives again," Xavier said, glancing around like he was…scared? Did anything actually scare a Master Vampire?

I had no idea what society he was talking about, but if it was enough to terrify a vampire as old and strong as this one, then I wasn't sure I wanted to find out. My skin prickled as the hairs on the back of my neck and arms stood on end.

He looked straight at me. "You would be wise to leave Miami as soon as possible. Come with me. I will protect you."

I let out an incredulous laugh. "Just not from you, right?"

He narrowed his eyes and smiled, his fangs brushing his bottom lip. "You would be far safer with me than them. Besides, I have information you want."

"I highly doubt that."

Jessa and the other angel approached him slowly, but Xavier paid them no attention. "If they found Maddox, then they'll find you, too."

My blood turned to ice, freezing me in place. I never wanted to hear my brother's name on those lips again. "Who?"

"You'll have to come with me to find out."

The sound of scraping shoes and a multitude of mutterings and growling gave us a whopping one second's notice before a dozen or so walking corpses rounded the corner.

The Risen.

Without a second thought, I drew a knife with my good hand and threw it, the blade finding a new home in a rotting forehead. The corpse went down. I took out another knife for close combat as the dead bodies kept coming, their skeletal arms reaching for me and the angels. This fight would be interesting with a broken wrist.

The second angel dropped the chains, too long to wield properly, and drew a massive broadsword from thin air. He bowed before each corpse that approached before decapitating them one by one in a single swing. Jessa distracted a few by slowly backing up or flitting away before landing again. Although she would have been trained to fight, her primary job was a healer, and they usually didn't mix tasks unless they absolutely had to.

I slammed my blade into a Risen's temple, then pulled it back out, letting the body collapse to the sidewalk. Bony fingers dug into my broken wrist. I cried out and punched the dead man in the side of the face with my knife's hilt. The move kept his mouth away from my skin long enough that I could flip the blade around one-handed. I thrust the blade upward into his brain by way of his jaw.

After carefully pulling my wrist free of his loosened fingers, I glanced over to where Xavier had been standing to see how he fared, only to find him gone.

My heart sank into my stomach.

The Master Vampire had fled into the night, taking the knowledge of my brother's murderer with him.

CHAPTER 17

Monday Night

When the dead were really dead again and bodies and body parts lay all around us, I whirled to face Jessa, wincing as I jostled my broken wrist. "How does he know who killed my brother?"

She took my wrist in her hands, her blue-green eyes uncertain. "I honestly don't know."

The other angel collected the iron chains he dropped earlier. "I've called for a cleanup crew, but I need to discuss this incident with Adam directly." He gave me a quick nod before launching into the air, his beating wings stirring up debris on the ground and throwing my hair in my face.

"Why didn't your friend save any of them to track the

mages responsible?" I asked, watching the other angel disappear into the night sky while I pulled strands of hair from my mouth and eyes with my free hand. My other wrist warmed and glowed faintly beneath Jessa's hands as her healing magic took hold.

"The connection was severed when they arrived," she said, letting go of my arm once the bones fused themselves back together. "The necromancer turned them loose when we were in their sight."

I gripped my knife tightly, wanting to slash something in my anger. The Master Vampire had information I needed, information that Adam refused to tell me, and now he was gone. There was zero percent chance I would have gone with him, but if the angels hadn't come along, maybe I could have tortured the information out of him before I dusted him.

Would he have even dangled that carrot in front of me had the angels not arrived?

I realized Jessa was staring at me, so I twisted my healed wrist a few times to check the range of motion. Perfect. "Thank you. Now, how the hell did a necromancer raise another horde of corpses? And this time they were just waltzing around the Miami streets."

Jessa frowned, her eyes deep in thought. "If Xavier is correct, then the Society of the Dead has come back. Adam will be most distressed."

"Oh, Adam will, huh?" I scoffed, though my frustration was most definitely not directed at her. "What is this Society? Besides the obvious."

Jessa sighed, her pearlescent wings fluttering against her back. "The Society was alive and thriving during the Dark Ages, operating with the goal of controlling everyone and everything. They have been forbidden to practice since the sixteenth century when we finally regained the upper hand. As far as I know, the Society has all but died out as the necromancers failed to pass on their knowledge."

"So how does a necromancer society suddenly pop up again without anyone noticing?"

"I don't know," Jessa said, her expression troubled.

My thoughts tumbled over each other, pushing to get out in front. A society thought long dead had sprung back to life without catching anyone's attention. Except something like that—training new mages in the art of necromancy—didn't happen overnight, which meant this had been planned for a long time. Like, for years.

As far as I knew, the agency still hadn't figured out Xavier's connection with the mages. Considering the fact that he was about to flee the area, were the Risen tonight coming after me, or the vampire? I wished I knew someone with more insider information since a certain brooding reaper loved to hold out on me.

Maybe I did know someone…

"Do you know Colin Ó Broin?" I asked.

Jessa's eyebrows pulled together. "The fae?"

"Yes." I breathed a sigh of relief. "Is he working with Adam on this necromancer stuff?"

"Not that I'm aware of," she said. "He requested a meeting with Adam, but I don't believe it's occurred yet. Adam's been very busy with this situation."

So, they were both lying to me. Colin implied he had already met with Adam and was working with him, and Adam said he didn't know who Colin was. I supposed Adam might not have been totally lying if he hadn't met with the fae yet. But why would Colin be trying to lie to me, and was that even possible? Was he trying to impress me?

My nostrils flared. This was *not* the way to do it.

Jessa gave me a quick smile. "You should get somewhere safe. I'll stay and cloak the fallen until Nathan returns."

I tucked my knife away, officially not angry enough to stab anything anymore. I was, however, more confused than ever. Careful to avoid bones and spilled guts, I stepped through the gore littering the sidewalk to collect my other knife from a cracked skull.

"Thank you for coming," I said as I tucked the blade away. Everything would need a good cleaning, myself included. "I'm not angry at you."

"I know." She shooed me away.

I turned and headed in the direction of my penthouse once again. A tickling sense of unease continued to agitate my limbs, keeping the hairs on the back of my neck standing on end. I looked back, but Jessa was standing serenely under the light of the moon and streetlamps, her magic keeping any cars passing by from taking notice of her wings or the carnage spread around her. An odd sight, even for me.

Shaking my head, I kept walking. But the farther I went, the worse the feeling got. My stomach roiled with anxiety.

Jessa yelled out behind me.

I whirled around, knives in hand. A fresh wave of Risen had her surrounded, at least a dozen of them, and more kept coming. Where the fresh fuck had these come from?

No time to figure that out just yet. I threw both my knives as I sprinted back to the angel, crunching followed by thuds indicating the blades found their marks. As I closed in, I pulled another knife free, this one better suited for close quarters. I stabbed a Risen in the back of the head as soon as I could reach. The skull crumbled beneath my blade, allowing swift access to the brain, and the body dropped like a stone. More stumbled in to take its place. Volume might end up being the biggest problem with these things, especially without Nathan's giant sword.

"Meet me in Adam's office," Jessa said as she spread her wings, "the fastest way you can get there." She launched herself into the air.

I didn't hesitate. With hands still reaching for me, I shifted to my falcon form. Teeth gnashed together, just narrowly missing my feathers as I followed the angel into the night sky. From the air, the DEA headquarters was easy to spot as it was one of the few office buildings with all the lights still on. Ten stories of glass windows lit up like a homing beacon.

By the time we landed on the terrace of Adam's office, the whole building seemed to be in frantic disarray. Adam stood behind his massive mahogany desk on a cell phone while reapers ran in, dropped papers and folders off, then ran back out, not even giving us a glance. Two reapers sat on the floor by the shelves, books spread out around them as they scoured page after page.

"What's going on?" I asked Jessa as we stepped inside the room, keeping out of the way.

"I'm beginning to sound like a broken record," she said, "but I'm not entirely sure."

My cheek twitched, but now was not the time to grin.

When the archangel ended his call, we approached his desk.

"Adam, another wave of the Risen attacked after Nathan left," Jessa said.

"I feared as much." His face was grim. "I've called for a lockdown. All angels and reapers are to return to the building immediately."

Bringing everyone back here meant no souls would be collected until the reapers were allowed back out again. That sounded like a terrible idea. Souls only had a limited amount of time to be collected before they disintegrated along with the bodies, their chance of moving on to a better place gone.

"Don't you think that's a little extreme?" I asked.

He glanced sharply at me but didn't seem angered by the question. "You were not the only ones ambushed tonight."

"How many others?" Jessa asked.

"Seven attacked, and we lost one of the reapers."

My lungs constricted just as Jessa gasped. After seeing Thane in action, taking down the manticore then the vampires when we faced Xavier, I had come to think of reapers as all but invincible. How many Risen had it taken to bring a reaper down? Or was a mage responsible? Had it been Thane?

"Who?" she asked the question I both needed and didn't want to know.

"Marcus."

I let out my breath as quietly as I could. I didn't want them to think I was relieved this guy died, but I was glad it wasn't Thane. For all that I was trying to avoid my feelings toward the man, I had come to like being around him. But also, I didn't want him to die when our last conversation had been an argument. I needed to make things right and clear the air before he could go and die on me. Die for real, anyway.

Plus, he was my best source of insider information. Jessa would never talk, and Colin was fudging the truth. I was positive I could squeeze some details out of the reaper.

"We're alerting all Community members to stay home and be vigilant," Adam said. "And we're working with human authorities already aware of the Community to control the threat when it arises."

Although the general Community population kept ourselves hidden from most of humankind, it was a benefit to find a few who could be trusted to maintain the secrecy. Community authorities like Adam worked with local humans when our existence threatened to come out or affect them somehow.

She probably already knew, but I sent Kit a quick text message to stay inside. She replied with a thumbs up. I would have to ask her how her date with Angela went once all this craziness settled down.

Adam's phone rang. "If you'll excuse me." He tilted his head toward the door leading out.

I followed Jessa into the foyer where I slumped onto the couch. We had gone from one wayward necromancer to an entire society almost overnight. And this particular Society had been very busy building an undead army right under everyone's noses before making themselves known. Just how big of an army remained to be seen.

"Has anything like this ever happened before?" I asked when Jessa sat beside me, her wings resting on the couch behind her.

"Not in centuries," she said, idly playing with some of her wing feathers. "The last uprising was the end of the Dark Ages."

"Were you an angel at that time?"

She smiled, her blue-green eyes twinkling. "A lady never reveals her age."

I chuckled. "Even to another lady?"

"With all due respect, V, you're not much of a lady." She winked at me and I laughed. She was completely right. I had no intention of becoming one, either.

"Why did the Society come back now?" I asked.

She sighed. "Honestly, I have no idea. I would have thought they learned their lesson the last time. Adam can be quite…motivating."

Right on cue, the archangel stormed out of his office. "Have either of you heard from Thane Munro?"

My heart dropped into my belly. "Not since earlier today."

Jessa shook her head, and Adam headed back into his office, throwing the door closed behind him.

I jumped to my feet and got to the door before it could slam shut. Ignoring Jessa's protests, I followed him inside. I didn't even care how against protocols or etiquette my behavior was. "Thane isn't here?"

Adam stepped behind his desk and checked something on his computer. "No."

"Where is he?"

"If I knew that, I would not have asked you." Adam's tone wasn't mean, but it was stern like answering a child who asked *why* for the fourth time.

I certainly didn't blame him; it was a pretty dumb question. But ghostly fingers had clamped around my throat, making it hard to breathe or think. "We got into a little… argument… earlier."

Adam snapped his head up to look at me directly. "Did he mention where he was going?"

I shook my head, my palms sweating.

A reaper rushed in at that moment. "Sir, Agent Munro's tracker deactivated about an hour ago. There's been no sign of him since."

CHAPTER 18

Monday Night

Fuck, fuck, fuck. Of all the times for my mouth to go and ruin things with Thane, it had to be in the middle of a rising zombie apocalypse. Thane was pouting like a petulant child after my comments earlier at Kit's, and now he wasn't checking in with his boss, a fact that made breathing a difficult task for me. That better be what he was doing at any rate, because if something bad had happened to him…

"Why wasn't I immediately notified?" Adam asked, his voice calm but tight with barely restrained anger, or maybe even fear.

The reaper gulped. "With all the Risen attack reports

coming in, we didn't see it until now."

The archangel pinched the bridge of his nose. "Jessa, please escort Ms. Neill home."

"Wait, I can help," I protested.

"You do not work for me, and you are not one for following protocols," Adam said, though his gaze softened slightly. "I will have Jessa let you know when Thane checks in."

Jessa dragged me out of the office by an arm before I could argue again.

"I want to help," I told her when we were in the waiting area. Sitting around doing nothing while someone needed help was worse than waiting in line at the DMV, and I wasn't very good at that either.

"You can help by staying safe and alive," she said, pushing me toward the elevators.

"I've done that fairly well so far."

She sighed as the elevator doors opened and we stepped in. "Have you already forgotten your last two encounters with Xavier?"

I pursed my lips. "I would have been fine both times."

"No, you wouldn't have," she said firmly as the doors slid closed. "You would have been reborn, sure, but he would have taken advantage of your momentary loss of control. You would have ended up a slave."

I mulled that around in my head as the elevator descended to the lobby. "I'm sure I would have figured something out. I'm pretty crafty when I need to be."

Jessa turned a hot glare on me and I almost took a step back. I hadn't realized I had riled her up so much, but I knew enough not to mess with an angry redhead, angel or not.

"This is not a game, Veronica." She balled her hands into fists. "I have spent most days of my life keeping an eye on you after we lost your brother. I will not let another man like Jackson take you from this world, too."

Her eyes opened wide and she quickly turned to face the door.

Holy shit. Did she just tell me the killer's name? The doors to the elevator opened and we stepped out into the lobby. I glanced at her out of my periphery and her face was still frozen in shock, her cheeks flushed pink.

Definitely an accident.

"Jessa, I—"

Whirling on me, her curly hair flared out around her like fire. She took my hands, her eyes pleading. "Please don't tell Adam."

My mouth popped open. I was surprised and also a little offended she thought I might. I was a semi-reformed thief, for flames sake—the farthest thing from a snitch. "Of course not."

She closed her eyes and a single tear slipped from one of the corners.

"Jessa, I won't. I promise." I squeezed her hands. "But thank you."

Her lagoon-colored eyes opened again and met mine. "You're going to get yourself killed if you do what I think you're going to do."

"But I'm going to try really hard not to, so that counts, right?"

She smiled, but her face still held a world of worry.

My phone rang. Colin. "Hang on, I'd like to take this before we leave."

She nodded.

"Yes?" I said into my cell.

"I've just been told what's happening," he panted like he'd been running. "Are you okay?"

"Depends. Adam tells me he's never met you."

A pause. "You've met with Adam?"

"Of course I have," I snapped. "*I* wasn't the one lying about that."

He sighed. "I didn't mean for it to be a lie. I need to meet with him on behalf of the prince. Adam hasn't fit me into his busy schedule yet." His voice was bitter.

"You said you were working with him on this whole Risen bullshit."

"That's the plan."

I pressed the fingers of my free hand to my temple, a throb threatening to start up. "I don't really know how to feel about this right now."

"I understand, but I hope you'll see I had really hoped to be working with Adam already by now."

"Did you think lying would impress me or something?"

"I didn't lie, nor would I have tried to impress you that way." He chuckled. "I didn't think Adam would refuse to see me when I came on behalf of Edric."

His response actually made sense, but I was still pissed. The fae weren't able to lie, which meant he was telling the truth. But I couldn't shake the feeling that he had tried to pull one over on me or something, and it had almost worked. Maybe I was more annoyed with myself for being so trusting of someone I just met.

"Please stay safe," he said after a lengthy pause.

"I'll try." I disconnected the call and sighed.

"More guy trouble, huh?" Jessa asked.

I made a face. "It can never be simple, right?"

She shook her head. "To be as safe as possible, I want you to fly home. I'm going to follow you."

I did as instructed, heading for my smaller apartment near the coffee shop, southwest of Brickell City Centre and just barely within the borders of Coral Gables. My penthouse downtown was nearer to the DEA but still a secret from most of the world including the angels, and I wanted to keep it that way.

The modern apartment building's white walls and glass-doored balconies were easy to spot as it was one of the taller residences in this part of the neighborhood. Balconies or terraces were a basic necessity when you lived part of your life coming and going as a bird. I had chosen a one-bedroom floorplan on the top level so keeping the balcony door unlocked wouldn't be a temptation for wannabe intruders. Not that it would have mattered too much with Kit's wards in place.

After a thorough search proved the apartment to be empty of any unwanted visitors—alive or dead—and still safely warded, the angel left to help with triage. I grabbed a package of Oreos and immediately called Kit, wasting no time when she picked up, "Hey, I need your help."

"The date was amazing, thanks for asking," she said, her tone sharper than I'd ever heard from her before.

I cringed as I sat on a stool beside the quartz kitchen countertop. The leather would be easier to clean than my couch if any blood or guts had followed me home. "Fuck, I'm sorry. Tell me about it and about her. Angela, right?"

"Tell me what you need."

I wanted so bad to just jump right into my story, but I was being a terrible friend. "It can wait. Where'd you go tonight?" I opened the Oreo container and shoved one in my mouth. The sugar would tide me over until I could eat a more substantial meal. Shifting and flying expended a ton of energy.

Kit paused, probably not expecting me to choose her over myself—a fact that made my heart clench even more—before she launched into a breathless story about how wonderful and magical her date was. So very unlike Kit. She was in love.

When she finally did take a breath a sleeve of Oreos later, I jumped in. "Did you tell her about you?"

She knew what I meant. "Fuck, V. Why can't you just let me enjoy the night first?"

"I'm not trying to ruin anything, it just sounded like you two were on your way to the altar already." I smiled because it was totally true. She was happy.

She muttered something into the phone. "Ridiculous, right? Too good to be true."

"No way, lady love. You enjoy this one until you can trust her enough. You deserve it."

Kit paused. "Thanks, V. For real."

"Now can we talk about me?"

She barked out a laugh. "Don't ever change, okay?"

"I'll try. But I found out the name of the guy who killed Maddox." A chill swept through me just mentioning it. I was so fucking close to some real answers.

"Whoa," she said. "Okay you definitely shouldn't have let me go on and on about my date."

"Aren't I such a good friend?"

"The best. Who is he?"

"I only got a name—Jackson." His name felt gross on my lips, fuzzy like I hadn't brushed my teeth in a few days. The coating of creamy Oreo filling didn't help. "No clue if it's a first or last name."

"I can work with that, give me a second." The click-clack of her keyboard filled the otherwise silent line. "Interesting. Jackson Reed. He's a realm-walker."

"A what?" I was fairly certain I had never heard the term before.

"He can move between any of the supernatural realms at whim."

Interesting indeed. Most realms other than the human one only allowed its own kind through the portals. Guests had to be accompanied by a host, with the exception being angels, of course. There were rare and dangerous spells that could grant one entry, but most people wouldn't go to the trouble. Besides, the practice was highly illegal, like necromancy—but look how far that got us.

"Anything else?" I asked.

"No, his record has been scrubbed clean, doesn't even say he was charged and convicted with anything. I might be able to find some more details, but it's going to take a few hours."

"Okay, well while you're doing that, I need you to also figure out how to get me into the prison without actually breaking in."

After I ended the call with Kit, I took a shower. Fighting off Xavier and the Risen had left my clothes a mess and my skin covered in gore. While the scalding water did its thing and scoured the blood and grime from my body, I let my mind wander over everything I had seen and heard recently, trying to put together a puzzle that didn't want to fit.

Everything except one possibly missing reaper, anyway. If my racing pulse was any indication, I wasn't ready to think about him again just yet. But we still didn't know why the necromancers had sent a group of Risen to help Xavier escape from the DEA, nor why the Society of the Dead had decided to come back out of the closet.

Why anyone actually enjoyed raising the dead was beyond me, but I did understand a thing or two about being drawn to illegal activities. The thrill of placing myself in dangerous positions, my heart pounding as I slipped past security systems and guards, was intoxicating and addicting. I missed it.

But that was about to change thanks to the case with Tabitha. I turned off the water and stepped out, wrapping myself in a towel as a smile tugged at my lips. Locating a wedding band with magical powers that Luka refused to return seemed like a fantastic distraction at the moment.

After finishing in the bathroom and getting into my pajamas, I sat in bed with my computer across my lap. Once I got some answers from Maddox's killer, I would steal the ring right out from under the alpha werewolf's nose. Tonight I would do some digging into the wolf pack leader's habits and history, a thought that brought back chills of anticipation and adventure.

Oh, how I had missed that feeling.

CHAPTER 19

Tuesday Morning

Kit's solution for getting me into the prison was so incredibly simple: she forged an order from Adam giving me access to the prisoner for questioning. No real break-in needed, and they would be hard-pressed to track the request back to her and her master hacking skills. I loved that girl's genius.

Isaac had messaged that he got my midmorning shift covered at the coffee shop, a fact that didn't really bother me anymore. If he wanted to play the petty man with a bruised ego, he was welcome to it. I sure as fuck wouldn't be apologizing to get my job back. All seven levels of hell would freeze over first. Besides, now I had plenty of time to pursue other activities, like confronting Maddox's killer.

I wasted no time driving the two hours to the prison, which had been built as far from civilization as the agency could get in southern Florida. Flying would have been faster, of course, but it would also leave me hangry—a disastrous combination of hungry and angry. I wanted to be at full physical and mental capacity to face this guy.

If you wanted to get technical, I shouldn't have left the Miami area, or even my apartment, due to Adam's lockdown order. Alone in my car with no one to bear witness to my inner struggle, I cringed with guilt. I was totally taking advantage of the chaos and exploiting the crisis, but could anyone really blame me? This was the perfect time to get some answers since no one else wanted to offer them.

After I parked, I took a moment in the car to calm myself. A few deep breaths in, a few deep breaths out. Today was the day I would face Mad's killer. Today I would find out why the motherfucker took him from me. I wouldn't be able to get the true justice I wanted and Mad deserved, but at least I would have answers. About fucking time.

Fuck you, Thane. My heart immediately leaped into my throat with the thought of the reaper, and I gripped the steering wheel tightly in both hands. Nope, not going down that path. He was fine. He had to be.

I took one last deep, unsteady breath before getting out of my Benz. Smoothing the creases from my blazer, I eyed the prison. High grey walls topped with barbed wire surrounded the entire fortress-like facility. Guards stood at every corner and patrolled the walkways between, reapers or hired guards of various species vigilantly watching the activities below. Unlike human prisons, however, a wavering glow encased the entire building—intense protection wards designed to fend off any outside attacks and keep those within from escaping.

As far as I knew, no one had ever successfully escaped.

Not that it mattered today. I had no intention of letting this guy be the first. On the contrary, he could rot in there for the rest of his life, and I hoped it was a really long life. I would even be happy if he got into a prison fight that led to some sort of nasty infection that drew out his death with intense pain for a while.

Either way worked, I just wanted my answers first.

After pressing the button outside the large metal door with an entrance sign above it, I followed the directions listed on a plaque and stated my name and reason for being there. A moment later, the door unlocked and swung forward on an automatic hinge. I stepped inside a long, windowless hall that ended a few yards down at another thick metal door. The one behind me swung shut with a clang loud enough to rattle my bones and the unmistakable sound of a deadbolt sliding into place. I swallowed hard.

I made my way down the hall, noting the multitude of cameras following my every step, and stood before the other door which had no handle, no signs, and no button. Was I supposed to knock?

Before I raised my hand all the way, the door clicked and swung open, and I stepped inside the prison's visitor reception area. I had expected it to be cold and uninviting, much like the outside, but it was quite the opposite. Warm hues filled the area, from the cream-colored carpet to the light blue walls. A few dark blue leather chairs sat to one side of the room, magazines on a small table between them, and a door with a bathroom sign above it stood opposite the seating.

Floral paintings hung from the wall behind the receptionist's desk, the receptionist himself being a glaring troll of a man and the only uninviting aspect of the room. I guessed he would be an easy six-foot-five when standing and was most likely an actual troll, though I wasn't sure why he would be glamoured to look otherwise. I would have thought facing a troll's ugly face would keep most people thoroughly afraid of making a wrong move.

The muscles of his dark brown arms stretched the fabric of his uniformed shirt close to ripping, his biceps almost as wide as my thighs. He was bald, but thick black eyebrows hung above equally dark eyes. Eyes that were laser-focused on me. I held back a gulp and stepped forward, glancing at his badge—Officer Harris. I decided to think of him as Officer Friendly for shits and giggles. I almost laughed except that would most likely not go over well.

"Hi, I'm Veronica—"

"You already provided your name," he cut me off with a deep baritone voice. "Sit and wait."

I did as I was told. As much as I wanted to act imperious with Adam's fake blessing for being here, I also knew not to rock the boat. If they contacted him to check the validity of his order, I would be kicked to the curb, and Adam would be beyond pissed.

Thankfully, I only had to wait a few minutes, not long enough to go into full panic mode. Officer Friendly called my name and buzzed me through a door behind him. The system showed I had access to the prisoner and voilà, I was in. The rising zombie apocalypse made for an excellent accomplice.

After following another behemoth of a guard down a series of windowless hallways, I stood in front of another large metal door which clanged and groaned as it fought to slide open. The prisoners here must not get enough visitors to warrant a little lubricant. I swallowed down another nervous giggle at the innuendo.

The guard ushered me inside the room, divided in the middle by a set of desks, ten total. Each had a chair facing a thick plexiglass window that kept us on one side and prisoners on the other, and dividers that gave a small semblance of privacy. I sat in an uncomfortable plastic chair—presumably made that way to avoid long visits—and waited, trying to ignore my racing pulse and the ominous groaning as the door slid shut once again.

No backing out now.

The door on the other side of the plexiglass opened and a guard walked in, followed closely by a prisoner in iron chains. My eyes narrowed as I assessed the guy who had taken my brother from me.

His dark brown hair had seen better days, but even sweeping past his chin in a choppy cut he may have done himself, the strands were full and wavy. From where he shuffled toward me, his hands and feet manacled close together, his eyes appeared a bright blue. Tanned skin peeked out from beneath his orange prison uniform.

All in all, Jackson Reed wasn't a bad-looking killer, which made me hate him even more. I gripped the arms of the chair, wishing it was a material I could sink my nails into.

I would never know what Maddox would look like as a full-grown man, and it was all thanks to this asshole.

The guard led the prisoner to the seat in front of me and unhooked the chain that kept his hands pinned together, though everything else remained heavily chained. Iron kept him from using his realm-walking ability.

Jackson lifted the phone receiver on his side of the glass and held it to his ear. I did the same.

"Well, isn't this the most pleasant surprise," he said, eyeing me behind the partition, which was in desperate need of a deep clean. He licked his lips. "Is this a conjugal visit?"

My temper was definitely going to get the best of me soon, but I had to keep it together for at least a few minutes. Someone was bound to be listening, and I didn't want to get thrown out before I got my answers. "I'm here because the agency has reopened a case. Someone you killed."

"Dirty talk before the act?"

"Maddox Neill." I watched his face carefully, and I'm glad I did. If I hadn't, I would have missed the slightest flicker of fear pass through his eyes.

"Interesting," he said. "Why?"

"He was my brother."

Jackson leaned back in his chair, his chains clinking together. A smile formed on his lips. "Ah, most interesting. The elusive Veronica Neill, I presume?"

I glared at him. "Why did you kill him?"

"You have really grown into yourself." He tilted his head to the side as he appraised me again. "Back then, the picture showed an angry little girl in need of a good spanking."

"Answer the question." My pulse raced as I fought to keep my anger and disgust in check.

"It wasn't personal, doll," he said with a smirk. "Just a job. I knew I'd end up here."

"You agreed to murder my brother knowing you'd be caught?" I shook my head. "That makes no sense."

"Maybe not to you, but I wasn't supposed to get caught until after I cut your pretty little throat, too." He grinned. "Good thing I negotiated to still get what I wanted out of the bargain, eh?"

I blinked at him, my mouth going dry. "You were supposed to kill both of us? Why?"

"Because you're a threat to them."

"To whom?"

His gaze turned thoughtful. "Is it possible you don't know who you truly are?"

I clenched the phone tighter in my hand, wishing I could bash the man's head in once I had my answers. "I know who I am."

He shook his head. "Ah, I see it now. You *think* you know, but there's so much more."

"So educate me," I spat. Why did everyone love playing these guessing games with me? "And what the hell did you get out of the *deal?*"

The door on my side of the plexiglass slid open, allowing three oversized guards to step in and approach me. Jackson tsk-tsked on the line as one of the guards took the phone from my hand and replaced it on the receiver—I'd been caught. Angry tears pricked the corners of my eyes.

"We'll escort you out," the guard said, his expression stern.

"That's it? I'm not in trouble?" My voice trembled as I struggled not to explode in rage. I followed him toward the door and cast one last look at the man who had taken my life from me. Jackson grinned as he stood, then blew me a kiss. My stomach churned in revulsion.

"The Archangel of Miami could not be reached earlier," the guard said, and the door to the visitor's room slid shut behind us with a groan and a clang. "But he has since returned our call and revoked your access to the prisoner. I'm sure he'll be in touch with you soon."

After he escorted me all the way to the parking lot, the air outside the prison threatened to smother me. I loved the heat and humidity, but right then, I felt like I was drowning in the thickness. I was beyond frustrated that I kept getting answers in bits and pieces.

What the hell did Jackson mean when he said I didn't know all of who I was? I definitely knew I was the last of my kind, and that could be quite the debilitating thought if I dwelled on it for too long. Yes, my genetics would pass on to any offspring I produced, but it was a lonely road until then, and way too clinical for my liking.

But what I didn't know—and the mere thought that there was more to who I was—left me with a feeling of raw vulnerability. I hated it. Why would anyone want the last of the phoenixes to die? What could anyone possibly get out of that? Who the fuck called in a hit on my brother and me?

I drifted to the car, lost in my thoughts and feelings, unsure of what I truly felt. As I slid behind the steering wheel, I realized I needed comfort. I needed someone to hold me and stroke my hair and whisper to me that everything would be okay, even though it was far from okay.

I lifted my phone and saw a text from Colin, but it wasn't the fae who invaded my thoughts. Thane's face had immediately popped into my head. I pulled up his number and called him. The phone went straight to voicemail. My heart sank toward my stomach, into an empty pit of despair.

Where the hell did that beautiful reaper go?

CHAPTER 20

Tuesday Afternoon

The meeting with Maddox's murderer must have rattled my brain and common sense, because the next thing I knew, I held the steering wheel in a death grip as I drove toward Luka's house. As in the alpha werewolf. What I intended to do, I wasn't entirely sure just yet. But I had to do *something* productive right now before a certain redheaded angel showed up ready to throttle me, or else I would explode.

Was I really doing this without any real preparation other than a handful of internet searches? Apparently so, but then again, I was never completely unprepared for anything.

I parked a few miles away on the side of the road,

outside the pack's perimeter. After removing the blazer I had worn for the prison meeting to seem more official, I folded it and placed it on the passenger seat. Thankfully, I had worn flats, so I didn't need to worry about running around and breaking into places barefoot. Nothing killed the mood like a nail in the foot.

To help mask my scent on jobs, I always kept field wipes in my glovebox. I used more than a few to wipe down my skin, hair, and clothes. Wolves had unbelievably powerful scent receptors, so I also scooped up some dirt and grass and smeared them all over my clothes and arms. The dry cleaners were going to have a field day gossiping about my recent escapades.

I hadn't brought any silver weapons with me, but that was probably a good thing. I didn't want to kill any of the wolves, although it would be nice to have the ability to threaten someone if I got caught. Okay, so I better not get caught. But I still tucked a few sheaths and knives, kept in my glovebox during the prison visit, beneath my clothes— enough to be prepared for a fight but not enough to say I was looking for one. Then I snagged a few explosives from the trunk; I always kept some extra supplies for my jobs either on me or in my trusty Benz.

When I was as prepared as I could be on a whim, I shifted into my falcon form and took to the skies. For a few minutes, I just enjoyed the warmth of the sun against my feathers. What I was doing was more careless than I preferred, but I did sneak in a bit of homework since my meeting with Tabitha the day before.

I knew the pack would be gone for most of the day since they all had jobs, like the majority of the Community.

There were some super wealthy outliers amongst our kind, like me, but not as many as you would think. Blending in required discretion, and a hefty bank account was the opposite of discreet for most people.

After a few swoops around the house showed no activity, I landed half a mile away in a copse of trees and shifted back into human form. Chances were there were some wolves inside the house or hidden nearby, but there was also a good chance they hadn't looked up to see the flame-colored feathers on the underside of my wings. Regardless, I still needed to deal with any lookouts.

I placed one of the explosives and lit the fuse, then took to the air again.

Thankfully, Luka lived on the outskirts of Miami, tucked away from any neighborhoods and surrounded by thick foliage, because the boom of the explosion shook the area and sent local birds flying. If any humans heard the blast, I wouldn't have long before fire trucks arrived.

As expected, two wolves sprinted out of the house and into the tree line to assess the potential threat. I dove down to the side of the building and shifted back into human form beneath a window. My heart thudding, I took a deep breath, then stood and reached for the window ledge. Landing on the sill as a bird would have been far easier, but far riskier now that everyone knew I could shift into a falcon. The house was on stilts, but I was still able to pull myself up enough to peek inside the window.

A bedroom, door shut, no one inside. Perfect.

After grabbing a nearby log—one of the reasons I had chosen to approach this side of the house—I placed it beneath the window and stood on it. The added inches gave me just enough height to shimmy the window open. No need to lock it when you lived in Bum Fuck, Egypt. I pushed the pane as high as I could while on tiptoes, then pulled myself inside.

I landed in a crouch, silent from years of practice. The flats helped, too. I stepped quickly but quietly around the room to gauge where I was in the house. A few picture frames covered the dresser, each drawer filled with a man's clothes. After a quick peek into the adjoining bathroom and finding it stocked and used, I determined this was the primary bedroom—Luka's. Talk about luck.

If I were hiding a pack-owned heirloom, it would definitely be in my bedroom. He would never expect anyone to break in and steal anything from him, not when his house was under constant surveillance.

Near-constant, anyway. I smirked.

My footsteps didn't make a single floorboard creak as I moved toward the bedside table and pulled out the drawer. A simple gold ring nestled in a corner. Bingo.

"Don't even think about it," growled a deep voice at the door.

Quickly palming the ring, I spun around to face Luka. "When kids are involved, I think about it."

Before I had a chance to shift forms and escape, his hand was at my throat, pinning me to the wall. Damn, he was *fast*. The muscles of his forearm twitched as he restrained himself from crushing my esophagus, which he could easily do. His hold didn't mean I couldn't shift, but I also had other tricks up my sleeve if I needed to use them. But first, words.

"She wants the ring for her son," I said even though his

hold was starting to choke off my air supply.

He leaned in close, his golden eyes smoldering with fury. Warm breath fluttered across my skin as he exhaled forcefully from his nose, bringing with it the scent of rain and wet pine. If I was positive he wasn't going to kill me in the next few minutes, I'd have enjoyed the smell enough to want to bottle it up for later. With his free hand, he grabbed my wrist and squeezed until I opened my fist. The ring clattered to the floor.

"I don't care who or what she wants it for," he growled. "The ring belongs to the pack. And if you have any hope of surviving after this encounter, you will convince Tabitha to return."

I nearly crumpled to the floor when he removed his hand from my throat and took a step back.

"You're letting me go?" I asked, rubbing my sore neck. I had expected to fight my way out if Luka showed up.

"As the alpha, it is beneath me to go to her and ask her to return," he said, his expression still seething with barely restrained anger.

"You mean beg."

A flash of his wolf rose beneath his face like a ripple, but he suppressed it. The beast wanted out to play, but the man had total control. Whoa.

"You are on thin ice, Falcon," he said between clenched teeth. "You will convince her to come to me, or I will have the pack hunt you down like the thief you are."

His words didn't hurt my feelings—I had worked hard to become the thief I was. The ring rested right beside my foot. I could bend down, pick it up, and fly away. The only trouble being his incredible speed. Damn it. Though to be fair, him giving me an out was the best possible outcome for getting caught.

"Deal."

He growled, low and menacing, making the hairs on the back of my neck stand on end. "Do not mistake this for a *deal*. You will do as I say, or you will die."

I raised my hands in surrender. "Yes, sir." The temptation to salute him was great, but so was my desire to live.

Luka stood there, fury radiating from him, and it took me a moment to realize he expected me to leave. I dropped my hands and shifted into falcon form, swooping out the window.

Back at my Benz, I used more wipes to remove as much dirt from my skin as I could before heading toward downtown Miami. As I neared my smaller Coral Gables apartment, I stopped for a quick burrito, a mouthwatering medley of steak, avocado, and spices. The sun was beginning its descent toward the horizon by the time I arrived home. I unlocked the door and let myself in, coming face-to-face with a very angry Jessa.

"You have gotten us both into a lot of trouble," she said, her opalescent feathers fluttering in agitation behind her. "Adam wants you in his office."

I felt bad that she was in trouble for my actions, but I didn't feel bad in the slightest for what I did to get into the prison. People were hiding things from me and frankly, it was pissing me right the fuck off.

"Tell Adam I'm busy trying to figure out what the hell he's hiding from me," I said as I laid my purse on the small table by the door.

"It wasn't a request," she said, putting her hands on her hips.

"Why the hell am I so important to him? To the agency?" Somehow, I kept my volume to just below screaming. Getting the neighbors riled up was the last thing I needed to add to my overflowing plate. Besides, it wasn't Jessa's fault.

"You'd have to ask Adam that, which means you need to come with me."

I had to give the girl some props—she was holding her own against my tantrum. I raised an eyebrow. "And if I don't?"

"He'll send a few of the not-so-nice angels to collect you." Her blue-green eyes narrowed as she looked me over. "Why are you so filthy?"

I rubbed my temples, the familiar throb starting to build with the stress of the day. The week. As much as I wanted to dig in my heels and show Adam he didn't have control over me, I also really didn't want to wreak any more havoc than I already had in the middle of a possible necromantic apocalypse, especially with Thane missing.

Besides, having Adam on my side would be far better in the long run. I needed answers.

"Fine, but only because I want to," I said, as if it made a difference. I might have been nursing a bruised ego after my failed theft. "And I fell."

Jessa rolled her eyes and practically stomped over to the open balcony. Her angelic cloaking magic would ensure no one saw her take off and fly away, and I would just look like a bird. Neighbors might even find my brown and grey outer feathers familiar.

Adam paced in his office, looking even more like a linebacker than usual with his fierce glare and biceps rippling as he clenched and unclenched his fists. His white wings twitched every few feet with distress. After a quick glance at each other once we landed, Jessa and I entered the room.

To my complete bewilderment, Adam let out a huge sigh of relief when he saw me and ran a hand over his face. "Oh, thank the Lord Almighty." He turned a stern look on Jessa. "She doesn't leave your sight again."

Jessa nodded, her lips pressed tight together.

"It's not her fault," I said. "I promised her I would stay put."

"Yes, and we know how well you keep your promises." He turned his glare on me.

Rude. He wasn't wrong, but like I've said before, I hadn't always been the bad guy. I had kept my promises once upon a time and still did when it suited me. "Why am I here?"

"We've found Thane," he said.

"Cool...?" I acted like I didn't care, but I was actually on pins and needles waiting for whatever came next.

Adam sighed. "The Society has him and they're trying to use him as bait."

My lungs fought for air as I blinked between the two angels. I finally managed to get out a word: "Fuck."

The side of Jessa's lip twitched but otherwise she remained as stoic as ever. Cursing in front of Adam was most likely a rare occurrence.

"His tracking device was found shattered in his apartment along with a note outlining their demands," Adam explained.

I winced at the thought of his tracker being removed again, and this time by unfriendly hands instead of Kit's. At least reapers healed fast. "So we're going after him, right? I just need to get changed and armed properly."

Adam smiled at me, somewhat sadly. "*We* will be looking for him, yes. You will be staying here, under proper surveillance to ensure your safety."

"You brought me here to trap me?" My voice rose. Maybe I could add yelling at an archangel to my list of firsts.

"I knew you would want to provide your assistance, and we simply cannot allow that," Adam said. "Thane's death would be terrible, of course, but your loss would be devastating on so many more levels."

"This is ridiculous."

"Jessa will show you to your room for the time being."

"Absolutely not." I was getting more and more prepared to stand my ground with the archangel. I had done well enough on my own without his help. Well, without knowing about his help. Fuck. Technically I had been saved twice by the angels, and I had no real idea if I would have won without them. Double fuck.

I bit the inside of my cheek. Was I really helpless?

"How would you feel, honestly, if your involvement got Thane killed because the angels needed to save you instead?" Adam's eyes held a hint of steel.

I glared at him. "Then tell them to just worry about their own."

His features softened. "No."

"Why the fuck are you keeping information from me, Adam?" I demanded. "Information about me, about my family? Why am I so goddamn important to you?"

"Because the truth is dangerous, and…" he paused for a moment to stare out the window. "I made a promise."

I flailed my arms, beyond frustrated. "Fuck your promises. Haven't we discovered it's far more dangerous to keep things from me?"

Adam sighed, then nodded to Jessa. The other angel approached me, her eyes wary. But my shoulders slumped in defeat, my confidence rattled, and I let her lead me from the room.

I paced in my jail cell. The room was far from an actual cell, considering it was a guest room for dignitaries of foreign realms. A queen-sized bed, vase of fresh flowers, and a private bathroom made the place really quite cozy. Too bad I was too fucking pissed to enjoy it—they had all but glued the window shut.

I didn't understand Adam and why he wouldn't want someone strong and capable on his team to find Thane. Sure, I might have made some mistakes in the past that required some assistance, but I most likely would have come out alive. I didn't need his goddamn help.

The angels knew more about me than anyone, even more than I did. They knew the power that lived inside of me, begging to be used. Usually I kept it at bay to hide the full truth of what I was from the Community, but I could also lay waste to this so-called Society with one good blast.

I checked the door again. Still locked. I didn't actually expect it to be open now, but I also needed to keep my hands busy. I resumed my pacing.

When Jessa first dropped me off at the room, I had scoured the place—checked every floorboard, every vent, looked through each drawer—to see if there was any weakness that would allow me a way out. I hadn't found a damn thing.

Think, Veronica. Thane had considered me caught when he had me in handcuffs, but I had used my phoenix fire to slide right through the metal. I glanced at the door. I could easily melt the knob and lock, but then I would have to fight my way through who knows how many reapers and angels— including Jessa. I cringed. No way. I was well and truly stuck.

My gaze caught my frustrated reflection in the window, and a spark of inspiration lit up my mind. I crossed the room and studied the frame. The metal was painted over, effectively sealing the whole damn thing shut. A few inches above the actual lock, giant screws were inserted into the frame to keep the window from rising more than a few inches. No person could come in and out once it opened.

But a bird could.

I pressed my palms to either side of the window and pulled my inner flame out to heat the paint. In a matter of moments, the paint bubbled and started to drip. I unlocked the window and pulled. It was stuck but giving way. I put all my strength into it, adding a little more heat to keep the paint melting but not enough to set the whole damned room on fire.

With a slight pop, the window opened until it smacked into the screws. I did a silent happy dance before shifting into my bird form and hopping out. I would have to keep my talons crossed that I hadn't set off any alarms.

CHAPTER 21

Tuesday Evening

With the warm night wind at my back urging me onward, I flew straight to Kit's in the dark and tapped on her window with my beak. She let me in, and I hopped down to the floor before shifting back into my human self.

"The necromancers have Thane," I said between gulping breaths. "They're using him as bait with Adam." Her eyes widened, but I kept going, "I don't have much time before Adam figures out I'm gone and comes looking. Will you help me find where Thane's being held?"

Without hesitation, she got behind her computer and started to work. I loved that girl and her beautiful brain even more at that moment. I made a quick pit stop in her kitchen to grab an apple from a fruit bowl before finding a place at her side. She had already pulled up maps and a bunch of other windows to figure this puzzle out.

"Okay, before it was deactivated, his tracker last put him here," she said, pointing to an area on a map near an executive airport. "That was yesterday, so he could be anywhere by now, especially if they took him on a plane."

I groaned then took a big, crunching bite of the apple. Fuji, my favorite.

"But my bet is that they lured him there because it's close to where they're preparing everything," she added. "Why else would he have been near that airport?"

"Good point," I said as I crunched. "Any guesses on where around that area makes sense for prepping to unleash a zombie apocalypse?"

She studied the map some more, then typed a few things into another window that looked like it was just code.

While she worked on figuring that out, I paced circles around her couch and ate my apple. My ping-ponging thoughts pulled me deep inside myself. I was so close to finding out why Maddox was killed, yet obstacles kept popping up left and right. If I went after Thane, there was a possibility, no matter how slight in my mind, that I would be caught and die. Perhaps even a real death if these necromancers learned what I was and knew the way to kill me. I was sure they could figure out a way to use my magic against me.

Was I prepared to die without knowing the full truth about Maddox's death and who we were?

The craziest part was that everything inside me

screamed yes, I was ready. Saving Thane was somehow more important than knowing the truth right now. Maybe because the reaper was here and "alive" while Maddox had already passed on. Whatever the reason, I didn't fully understand it, but I would listen.

If nothing else, Mad's killer was behind bars at a maximum-security supernatural prison. There would be no escaping. And while I knew now that Jackson Reed wasn't the one who wanted my brother dead, he was the one who made it happen. That would have to be enough for right now.

"This is insane if it's right," Kit muttered under her breath.

"What?" I ceased my pacing at the trash can and tossed the apple core.

"The Hard Rock Stadium has been closed for renovations again," she said, looking up at me. "It can hold a shitton of people and has a partial roof, which would hide their activities from view."

"You think they're hiding a bunch of dead people inside?" My stomach turned over at the idea.

"As crazy as it sounds, yeah, I do."

"It's worth a shot to check out." I headed for the open window.

Thousands, make that tens of thousands of Risen could be held in the stadium. The thing was huge. How they had accumulated so many bodies without anyone noticing was beyond my knowledge or concern right now. I also didn't have a clue what the necromancers planned to do with all those bodies—if they managed to Raise that many—but my guess was nothing I wanted to find out. Once I got Thane out of there, it would be back to Adam and figuring out the details.

Provided we survived, of course.

"Alright, I'm going to head to the penthouse to get suited up," I said, turning to Kit. "I'll make sure to keep my earpiece on."

"No need." She stood. "I'm coming with you."

I blinked at her. "You're what?"

"I'm going to help you. This mess affects everyone, not just you and Thane."

"As much as I appreciate the offer," I said, "there's no way I'm going to let you come with me. I love you too much to lose you."

Kit smiled. "Girl, I could kick your ass so fast you wouldn't know what hit you."

"I—"

"No more arguing. You're falling for Thane in a way I've never seen before, and you're going to get yourself killed with your rash, love-fueled decisions."

My mouth hung open. "I'm not—"

"Yes, you are," she said sternly. "I'm coming. End of story."

I regarded her for another moment. "Are you going to use magic again?"

She shook her head. "Necros are mages, humans who learned to control magic. I can handle that. And I've got a few tricks up my sleeve to show them how weak they really are." Her eyes gleamed.

"Okay then, let's go," I said.

"You fly straight there, I'll follow on the ground."

After another moment of hesitation, I rushed over to

her and hugged her. "Thank you."

Not exactly the hugging type, she patted me on the back. "See what I mean? You and your rash, love-fueled decisions. Now go."

I blew her a kiss before shifting into a falcon and swooping out the window. Now that we knew Thane had been captured, a strong sense of urgency drove me onward. As I angled for my penthouse, I prayed to all the phoenix gods and even the reapers' that we made it to him in time.

As soon as I landed on my terrace at the Brickell Flatiron, I shifted back to my human form and headed straight to my closet to change into my normal hunting gear—navy-blue cargo pants that were a slim fit but still loose enough to allow me to fight, a basic black tank top that wouldn't interfere with my holsters and belt, and boots sturdy enough to kick some ass while also allowing me to run when needed. Not all fights were worth having.

As I headed for my weapons cabinet, I pulled my long blonde hair up into a ponytail, then wound it around a few times and secured it into a bun with a few bobby pins I grabbed from the bathroom. The cabinet, which served as a pantry most of the time, hid my weapons behind the food shelves. I pressed the button—nearly impossible to find for anyone who hadn't used it before—beneath an otherwise-smooth shelf and opened the hidden storage racks.

I had no intention of fighting every single Risen, but I planned to arm myself to the teeth just in case. My goal was simple: sneak in, find Thane, sneak out. All without being noticed or killed. It wouldn't be that simple of course, but I would do my best. I always did.

Because we would most likely be dealing with a whole host of unknown entities, I decided to bring Lisa, the short sword I usually reserved just for demons. Her name came from the shared phoenix and Russian word for she-fox, because no one expected her to do as much damage as she was capable of in my hands. Sneaky little blade. I strapped on the leather sheath, placing the weapon along my left hip, and pulled the sword free to ensure she didn't need a last sharpen. Nope, she looked perfect as always.

Lisa would do the job well in up close quarters, but I hoped to avoid getting close enough to use her. I grabbed my shoulder holsters and strapped them on. A specially designed Smith & Wesson handgun that shot bullets which exploded with wooden shrapnel went into one holster in case we faced vampires, and a second that shot silver bullets went into the other. Nothing indicated werewolves were involved, but I would be prepared if they were.

Another holster went on my right hip, this one just a good old regular handgun for the Risen and their mages. I had a few magazines in one of my cargo pockets, and the bullets were spelled to go right through any defenses the necromancers might have. I would try regular bullets first because the magic ones were really hard to get my hands on. Illegal use of magic and all that. All three guns came equipped with suppressors to keep the flash and noise down.

As I added a variety of poisoned, wooden, and spelled knives to my arsenal, the song "Girls, Girls, Girls," by Motley Crüe popped into my head, only with the words "Knives, Knives, Knives." I had been training my entire life with just about every weapon including my hands, becoming more of a jack of all trades rather than an expert in each. But knives were my absolute favorite. They were easy to hide, yet with a sharp-enough blade and a well-aimed throw or thrust, just as deadly as anything else.

The front door opened and closed, and Kit popped around the corner right as I belted out the next verse in my song:

"Knives, knives, knives,
Long blades and a fatal kiss,
Knives, knives, knives,
Flyin' through the air tonight,
Knives, knives, knives,
Poison tips, death for some."

Kit stopped to stare at me, then shook her head. "Girl, you've got problems."

"If I can't serenade my best friend and soul sister before facing a horde of the undead and their nefarious masters, then I don't even want to live anymore," I said as I tucked another knife into the hidden sheath in my boot. I always got a bit anxious before a fight. Not nervous, but more super excited, and sometimes that came out in a giddy, inappropriate fashion. Hence the song.

Still shaking her head, Kit headed for the pub-height dining room table and set up her laptop. "Alright, when you're done having a moment, let's talk strategy."

I eyed the weapon racks one last time, lips pursed in consideration, before deciding I was ready. It was a good thing that the arsenal strapped to my body would stay put when I shifted into my falcon form, and even better that everything wouldn't weigh me down while I flew. After closing the cabinets, I headed to Kit and stood beside her. She had pulled up blueprints of the stadium, including all levels, exits, and even ventilation systems.

"I've been able to locate security camera footage near the area that the mages didn't find and disconnect." She pointed to an entrance on the map. "It's not perfect, but this area here has been less guarded than some of the others. According to the prints, it's a one-way emergency door that can only be opened from the inside or with a special key from the outside. No handle, so they probably don't bother to watch it."

"No handle, no problem," I said.

"Before we go in, I want you to do a few passes overhead to check for heat signatures. Find out where the Risen are concentrating and where the others might be."

I nodded, though I also chewed on my lip. Out in the open, reapers didn't emit any ultraviolet light, they were completely devoid of the stuff and almost seemed to leak darkness. Inside a building, Thane might be all but impossible for my avian eyes to see, but my phoenix genetics made it possible to pick out heat signatures. I would have to hope that something about their gatherings would indicate him being close.

That, or we would just have to kill them all and save the world. Woo.

"Any questions?" Kit asked.

I shook my head, and she closed her laptop and grabbed the messenger bag of supplies she had brought.

A grim smile pulled her lips into a tight line. "Let's do this."

CHAPTER 22

Wednesday Before Dawn

As predicted, the stadium's roof was closed as far as it could go, but the gap allowed my enhanced vision as both a falcon and phoenix to see the ultraviolet light and heat signatures beneath. The Risen were dead but animated, which meant they emitted a muted light. It was easy to see them gathered en masse on the outskirts of the field, but determining their number would be next to impossible. Although their light blended into one another's, the sheer size of the group said there were a fucking lot of them.

The necromancers had been busy building this crowd, but I had no idea where all these bodies came from. I hadn't seen any missing persons or bodies reports in the news, although I really wasn't looking either. But I would think *someone* at the DEA would have noticed. Maybe the mages robbed a few cemeteries and paid off the groundskeepers.

I took another loop, this time looking for heat signatures of guards and lookouts, taking note of how many stood at each entrance or paced the halls. Where the blueprints had indicated VIP suites would be, human body heat shone more brightly. That must be where the mages were meeting.

On my last swoop over, I checked for any oddities in the heat signatures—any places that hinted at warmth being sucked from its source, indicating a reaper's presence. It wasn't until I was about to give up and join Kit down below that I spotted what I hoped would be Thane: a tiny pinprick of darkness amongst the mages' bright light.

I held back the screech of victory I wanted to let out, not needing to draw any attention to my flame-colored underwing feathers, and landed beside Kit's motorcycle. She had parked just south of the stadium in a nearby residential neighborhood to avoid notice. I shifted back into my human form as she turned off the motor and swung her leg over.

"Can you pull up the blueprints again real quick?" I asked.

She pulled out her phone and brought up the prints. I pointed to an area marked for The Nine club. "He's here, but I don't think he's with the mages. What's below them?"

Kit turned the print to another page which showed the next level down. A storage room. Bingo.

"That's got to be where they're keeping him," I said, trying to keep myself from getting too excited. Things were going well so far, but we hadn't even entered the building yet. A horde of undead and their necromantic masters were still between us and Thane.

"Patrols inside?" she asked.

"There were a few patrols between the entrance we'll use and the storage room, spaced a few minutes apart, and a flight of stairs, but that's it," I said. "You ready?"

Kit tucked her phone away and nodded. After ducking through the neighborhood's tree barrier, the two of us ran across the normally busy 199th street, virtually deserted now in the predawn hour. Our boots kissed the asphalt in time with each other. We hopped over the chain-link fence surrounding the stadium's perimeter, and I was pleased to note Kit made as little noise as I did despite being the brains rather than the brawn of this operation.

I knew she had done some spy work back in the World War II era, but the girl hadn't lost her touch. Also, she was just as much brawn if she wanted to be.

As we snuck closer to the main stadium, we stayed close to shrubbery and the walls of the outer buildings and tennis courts. Miami nights were far from quiet, with the variety of musical bugs and the whoosh of random cars going by, but my pulse drowned out those sounds as it thudded loudly in my ears from the physical exertion and adrenaline. Twice we had to stop and wait for a patrol to pass by, and I took advantage of these quick breaks to breathe deeply.

From our distance and the lack of lighting, it was too hard to tell if the patrols were mages or hired mercenaries of another species. With how fast the Society came back to life and the size of the army of Risen they raised, the people passing us by could easily have been mages or even mage wannabes. Seeing so many in one place was beyond disturbing, and there were even more of the bastards inside. My skin prickled at the thought.

When we were a quick run's distance from the virtually hidden door, we stopped, crouching down behind some foliage. I had never been so thankful for Florida's abundance of robust plant life. I pulled out my lockpick case and the two tools I would need. A good thief never left home without a set.

"Let's wait for the next patrol to pass, then make a dash for it," Kit said, her eyes continually surveying the area.

I wet my lips, dry from the trek across the stadium's vast grounds, and tasted salt on my skin. Sweat dripped down my forehead and back, both from the humid air as well as my nerves.

The patrol passed by and we made our move. As soon as we reached the stadium wall, we ran our hands along the surface trying to feel for the cracks of the door. After a tense moment where I thought we had made a mistake, Kit found it. The outline was practically invisible against the white paint on the wall, and they had even painted over the lock casing to hide it.

I inserted my wrench and pick and got to work setting the pins. A few moments later, the lock turned and the door nudged toward us like it was on a spring. Before pulling it open all the way, I put my face to the crack and peeked through.

Only one direction of the hallway was visible, but it was also clear. We would have to take our chances. I looked at Kit, then nodded at the door before drawing my handgun loaded with regular bullets and attached silencer. No sense in wasting the specialty bullets if I didn't have to.

I exhaled, trying to quiet the pounding of my pulse, then pulled open the door and stepped inside with my arms outstretched and the barrel facing the direction I hadn't been able to see. Clear.

I waved Kit inside, then pulled the door closed behind her. It clicked shut. I led the way down the hall, keeping my gun up and ready to fire. Other than Thane, I didn't expect to find any friendlies within the building, so shoot-on-sight was my motto du jour. Kill or be killed. I might not have been a cold-blooded killer on a normal day, but as far as I was concerned right now, they took the first shot by kidnapping the reaper.

Our footsteps were as silent as ghosts haunting these wide, concrete halls. As we closed in on a sharp turn to get to the stairs, low voices echoed in the emptiness. I stopped at the corner and crouched down, peeking around the wall. Two men in blue security uniforms stood near the stairs. As much as I would have liked taking my time to properly stake the place out and learn the guards' habits like one of my regular cases, we simply didn't have that luxury.

I pulled back and stood. Holding up two fingers to Kit, I pointed to myself and the gun. She nodded. I would have to assume the guys were mercenaries and change my plan if they proved otherwise.

As soon as I turned the corner, I fired twice. I had spent my entire life training in scenarios like these, and I rarely missed. The first man went down, a bullet through the middle of his forehead. The second dove to the side and my bullet just grazed his ear.

His reflexes were impressively fast. He tumbled before

jumping to his feet and chanting two words. A mage. I pulled the trigger again, but the bullet embedded itself into a nearly opaque shield that materialized in front of him.

A bottle rolled across the floor to land at the man's feet, emitting grey smoke that immediately clung to his clothes, swirling around him as it climbed higher. He glanced down and drew a foot back to kick it away. Before he could finish the move, the smoke had traveled up his body to congeal around his face. Stumbling backward into a wall, he clawed at the blob covering his only source of air. Within moments, he slumped to the ground.

One of the tricks Kit kept up her sleeves—bottled magic. Nice. From the few conversations we'd had about the subject, I knew she was attuned to the fire and earth elements. The blob was an air elemental spell, so I assumed bottled magic allowed witches to tap into the other elements. The more I thought about it, my witchy best friend really did use magic still, just not in the traditional way.

The area was clear. The room where I thought they would be hiding Thane was up a flight then down another long hallway. My heart beat wildly in my chest as we approached the entrance to the stairwell, knowing how close we were but also how many more obstacles we might face.

I grabbed one of the mage's walkie talkies and turned the sound down to barely audible. Our window of time would grow even shorter if anyone checked in on the two guards we took down, but at the very least it would give us a heads up.

We entered the stairwell and climbed the steps, keeping to the wall and ready to act should we need to. One flight up, I approached the door to push it open. Another one creaked open directly above us and footsteps entered, made by several pairs of feet. They started to come down.

I met Kit's gaze and tilted my head to the door. We would have to take a chance and hope the next hallway was clear.

Pushing it open as quietly as I could, we slipped through and closed it behind us. The hallway was empty, and I let out a tiny sigh of relief. A scent I had vaguely noticed before grew stronger, like garbage left to rot in the sun. I scrunched up my nose, trying unsuccessfully to close my nasal passages from the stench. No such luck.

Resisting the urge to cover my nose with my shirt or hand, I led Kit in the direction of the storage room where I knew we would find Thane. My skin started to crawl with paranoia. I had hoped it would be this easy, but it shouldn't have been, unless the necromancers were too focused on something else to worry about two intruders. I mentally crossed my fingers since my real ones held a gun.

Two doors down from the storage area, one of them opened and a man wearing a black robe with red accents stepped out, facing me directly—a mage. Six more in similar getups and a handful of assumed mercenaries in military-style camo garb followed him out.

Our way forward, and to Thane, was blocked.

CHAPTER 23

Wednesday Before Dawn

You didn't really think we'd be dumb enough to just let people sneak in uninvited, did you?" the mage asked, a sneer making his ugly face even uglier. Since he was human, he didn't get the lucky benefit of having his features enhanced like other members of the Community.

"Yeah, actually, I did," I said with a small shrug.

The red splotches on his face darkened. Maybe I could rile him up enough to make an even dumber mistake.

"Take this bitch to William," he said. "Both of them."

Two of the mercenaries stepped forward. If I started shooting, the fight would begin in earnest, but I needed Kit out of there first. We needed backup.

"Kit, use your other powder stuff and run," I said out of the corner of my mouth. "Go get Adam."

"I'm not leaving you," she said, though she slid a hand into her bag to grab something.

"You know I'll be fine. *Go.*"

She hesitated for just a moment before she leaned close and whispered, "Your parents would be so proud of you."

Now, I was sure that sounded like the sweet remarks for someone heading to their death, and I wouldn't deny Kit had a tender moment there with the smile and all. But in reality, it was a secret phrase we came up with years ago to indicate it was the right time and place for me to go nuclear if I needed to.

She whipped out her hand and dashed the glass bottle at her feet. A thick, billowing black fog filled the spot where she stood, making the rest of us cough and wave our hands to clear the air. When it dissipated, she was gone.

That's my girl, I thought somewhat sadly. I didn't actually know if I believed myself when I told her I would be fine, but I sure as hell wouldn't let them hurt Kit. She would get Adam, and he and his angelic legions would lay waste to these imbeciles. Kind of sounded like what I should have done in the first place.

Ah, well. Hindsight. He never would have let me tag along, anyway.

I refocused on my gun and the men closing in, only to find myself frozen in place. While Kit's exit had distracted the majority of the mages and mercenaries, it had also diverted *my* attention, and one mage chose that moment to cast a spell on me. Dirty move, fucker. Like stabbing someone in the back.

The closest merc stepped forward and pulled my stiff arms behind my back. I winced as my limbs fought against both the movement and the magic holding them in place. Even though the device wasn't visible, the sound of a zip tie being pulled tight was unmistakable. After relieving me of Lisa and most of my other weapons—I had some hidden they'd never find unless they stripped me naked, which didn't seem likely just yet—the mage released the freeze hold on my body.

With only a plastic zip tie holding me, escape would be easy, but I needed to give Kit time to rally the troops. The mercenary who bound my arms pushed me down the hall and past the area where they were keeping Thane. I considered yelling to let him know I was here, but I didn't want him to try anything stupid. That had turned out to be my job.

After another flight of stairs up, I followed the mage through a door and gagged from the overwhelming stench of decaying bodies. The insides of my nostrils burned and my eyes watered.

"How the fuck do you guys stand this smell?" I asked, trying to pull my arms up enough to allow me to cover my nose or even tuck it into my armpit. It didn't work, and my stomach churned with nausea.

No one answered. When I could focus on anything other than my rising stomach contents, I looked up through still blurry eyes. A whole host of men and women in black-and-red ceremonial robes milled about, enjoying themselves with drinks in hand—a few dozen mages. Necromancers just enjoying a party. The area we entered was obviously how the filthy rich people attended football games, and I will be the first to admit, I planned to buy a few tickets as soon as I cleaned the vermin out. I, too, was filthy rich, after all.

A giant golden chandelier hung over the main bar and stretched into the room. Each piece of the artistic lighting contraption looked like the pipes from an organ—the musical kind, thankfully. The rest of the seating areas were decked out in browns, greens, and golds, and a palm leaf pattern. It was pretty, if not my personal style. Taking in the room allowed me to identify the various exits, including the glass doors leading out to the main stadium seating itself.

Eyeing the mages' robes with disdain, I shook my head. "You guys really need to stop playing into stereotypes."

The guard behind me pushed my shoulder hard, and I stumbled forward, unable to use my arms for balance. At least the spell that had frozen me in place had been lifted after they secured me.

I whirled back around to glare at him. "Pushing a girl while she's bound makes you a tough guy, huh?"

Taunting these people was probably not my smartest move ever, but I just couldn't help it. They had really pissed me off. If it hadn't been for their little uprising, I might have gotten more answers on Maddox's death already. But no, the dead just *needed* to be raised right now. For what?

I paused my mental tirade. I still didn't know why they were doing this.

The man who had pushed me focused on something over my shoulder and straightened, stepping back into line with his buddies. When I turned around, another black-and-red robed man stepped out of the group, a smile on his face that was most definitely not friendly. Cruel and malicious would describe it far better.

His long, silvery-white hair fell straight beside the dusky, blueish-grey skin of his somewhat-sunken cheeks, his eyebrows the same snowy hue as his hair. Ice-blue eyes flecked with silver gazed at mine, tiny creases forming at the upturned corners as he smiled. His build was slim to the point of being bony, almost sickly, but his lack of muscles didn't mean much. I could feel power radiating from him. He reached a hand up to tuck an errant strand of hair behind his ear.

His pointed ear—a fae.

What the everloving fuck? Since when did fae become necromancers? Was that even possible, or was he just the leader of the human mages? Not only that, but this man's coloration meant he was of the Winter Court, as in an *unseelie* fae. As in, shouldn't even be able to be in the human realm.

Millennia ago, when the realms were first connected, an agreement was made between the angels' god and the Summer King of the time: only fae of the Spring, Summer, or Autumn Courts may enter the human world. As in only the seelie, or the "good" kind of fae, if such a thing even truly existed. I was sure Joe or Colin could surprise me with some hidden evil tendencies.

"Welcome to our humble abode, Ms. Neill," the fae said, opening his arms as if welcoming me to his home. His power rippled over and through me like a cresting, frost-filled wave. "We're all so glad you could attend our gathering. It's going to be a special night, even more so now that you're here. I'm William Caomhánach, your host."

"Bill the Necromancer? You're kidding, right?" I asked, shivering as the last of his magic wave faded from my skin. Humor helped me keep a grip on the fear that was trying to take over my brain and body.

William's face darkened to a deeper grey, losing the deadly smile, and he clasped his hands in front of him. "Oh, we're going to have great fun together."

"I'm actually not all that into dead things," I said with a shrug.

"No?" His eyes took in the various weapons the guards took from me, lingering on the sword, before rising to meet mine again. "I thought you came to rescue a particular reaper. Pity."

"Are you actually raising the dead, as a fae?" I asked, not willing to rise to the bait.

"I am indeed."

My eyebrows skyrocketed toward my hairline. "Why? And how?"

"All in good time, Ms. Neill. First things first, you are going to help me with a special project." He crooked his finger as he turned, heading toward the front of the VIP area where the room opened up to view the field below. Floodlights were turned on and directed at the grass. He swept his arm out toward the undead mob milling around. "Behold, my army."

There were far more Risen than I had originally thought, like hundreds more. Either there were more mages learning necromancy than I realized, or they had in fact raided a few cemeteries.

"How did you raise so many without notice?" Genuine curiosity tinged my tone.

William flashed a sly smile. "I knew you'd get into the spirit."

He nodded at one of his followers, who muttered something into a walkie talkie. All around us in the sky boxes and suites, men and women stepped into view. There had to be at least fifty of them, many with the same dark grey skin as their leader. I never would have dreamed he would have so many mages at his disposal, *fae* mages, and these were just the ones he was showing me.

A few suites over, Frank Turner, the guy who owned the airboat tourist attraction, raised a cigar in my direction. I glared at him. That explained the tingle of magic when we shook hands. Maybe he really did have a Risen locked up on his property somewhere with his tracker stuck in it.

I pulled my attention back to the crowd of dead bodies below us. "I get it, you have the mages to do it, but how did you avoid notice by human or Community agencies? That many missing bodies is sure to attract someone's notice."

"In some areas of this beautifully naive country, the humans buried their dead right on top of each other," William explained. "Bodies upon bodies in a single grave."

I stared at him, my lip curling up in disgust. "You had them shipped in?"

"Some. There are still plenty of graveyards in this city, and humans and their memories are easily manipulated by money or magic."

I shuddered. "I thought necromancy died centuries ago."

"In the human world, it did."

I snapped my head to look at his ears. "How are you even doing this? I thought only human mages could perform necromancy due to magical restrictions or something like that."

"Nonsense told to help you sleep at night. Fae magic makes it exceptionally easy to raise a large number of the dead. And it had a number of unexpected but remarkable consequences." His eyes gleamed. "Would you like to see?"

I didn't want to admit it, but my curiosity was getting the best of me. Thankfully, the narcissist didn't actually expect me to answer. He raised an arm no thicker than my wrist out toward the field as some sort of silent signal. His blue irises darkened to inky black, spreading to encompass the entire whites of his eyes as well, his magic taking hold.

The grumbling and muttering of the Risen on the field grew louder as the horde turned as one to face us. Shivers shook my shoulders as goosebumps raced along my limbs. He had such control over these monsters, it was nearly unfathomable.

Dread began to build in my gut.

One by one, individual Risen separated from the group to stumble forward, pulling away from the rest. Dozens ended up forming a line in front of them, skin and other unpleasant things hanging from various parts of their skeletons. Some were just bones, only standing thanks to the magic holding them up. William turned his hand, still held out toward the field, in a circle.

A gruesome cracking sound split the air, sending the hairs on the back of my neck reaching for the sky. The Risen in front shifted and changed, morphing into other half-decayed creatures. Before my eyes, undead werewolves and shifters of all kinds—foxes, snakes, a boar, and even an enormous skeletal bear—raised hollow, still-dead eyes toward their master.

Holy fuck. We were all in big trouble.

CHAPTER 24

Wednesday Before Dawn

I couldn't help it, my mouth dropped open. Like, probably would have fallen straight onto the floor if it hadn't been connected to my skull. The crazy ass fae necromancer standing next to me had raised shapeshifter Community members, knowing his fae magic made it possible for them to shift forms even in death.

If I thought what Xavier and Sophia did to Broderick was blasphemy, then I didn't have a word for what this fucking shitshow was.

William caught my look and barked out a delighted laugh. "Ah, what a beautiful moment to share together. Shall we make it even more fun?" He turned to the mage with the walkie talkie. "Have them bring out our entertainment."

The mage bowed and spoke into his walkie talkie again. William's eyes retained their deep darkness as he exerted his control over the Risen. A door opened on the field, the one where the players would normally come bursting out. Instead, a bound and gagged man stumbled through, pushed by his captors until he reached the green grass of the field.

My boiling-hot phoenix blood chilled to glacier level in an instant.

That man was Thane. And he did *not* look good. They had tortured him. His shirt hung in rags off of his body, but instead of displaying his beautifully defined abs, red and black slashes caked his skin—both dried and fresh blood. Flesh gaped open in numerous places, not showing bones but weeping from lacerations. Purple, yellow, and black covered his face, and one eye was completely swollen shut. He panted against the gag as they forced him to his knees.

I balled my bound hands into fists behind my back, my nails digging in so hard that warmth accumulated between my fingers. His reaper magic should have healed anything they did to him, except it hadn't. What had they done to him? My fury rose quickly, but I needed to waste time, drag this whole thing out until Kit had a chance to call Adam for backup. The archangel was going to be *pissed*.

At least the whole necromancer thing would keep his rage focused on them for a while. Hopefully his anger would be subdued by the time he dealt with me. Wishful thinking, I was sure.

"What do you think, Ms. Neill?" William asked. "Will the reaper survive against an army of the Community Risen? Are their powers that strong?"

"Is that what this is about?" I asked as I turned to face

him. "Testing the powers of the agency?"

"Partly." His unnaturally black orbs met my gaze. "But mostly just for fun. We learned quite a bit about the reapers' strength when we let Xavier free."

I glared at him with as much hatred as I could muster, wishing with every fiber of my being that I could kill him with just my stare. "So he was helping you."

"Oh no," William said, his smile cruel. "Xavier was far from helpful. He and his creatures tried to stop my work on more than one occasion, even going so far as to kill Broderick."

"Broderick was helping you?" My mouth hung open in disbelief. If I wasn't careful with all this open mouth business, I was going to catch some flies. I forced my lips closed.

"Of course. Angelic magic would be far superior to even the fae's in Raising the dead. We let the vampire loose to hunt him down. Far more entertaining than a beheading, don't you agree?"

I just stared at him, trying to process everything he just said. "You let that monster loose for…sport?"

"William," said a man's voice from behind us all before the fae could respond. A voice I recognized. "We have a kink in our plans."

We all turned to face the newcomer, and my heart dropped to my stomach as my ears proved me right. "Colin?"

His blue-green eyes met mine, as confused as I felt. Frowning, he turned to William. "What is the meaning of this?"

"Oh, don't blame me," William said. "Your girlfriend

showed up on her own."

"You're with them?" I asked, my voice barely more than a whisper. Just my fucking luck. First I fall for a dead guy, then I start falling for a guy who Raises the dead. What the fuck was wrong with me?

"V, I can explain," he said, taking a step closer.

"Explain what? That you're a necromancer?" I scoffed, the brief sense of dismay burning up in my returning anger.

"The Death Enforcement Agency and our Summer Court queen have grown too strong, too overreaching," Colin said. "The people of our respective realms deserve better. The Society's goal is to bring both down and allow each Community type to build their own form of government, to live where they please."

I barked out a laugh. "You're kidding, right? The agency is overseen by the angels themselves. A bunch of dead corpses isn't going to do shit."

I couldn't care less about what happened to the stupid fae queen. As far as I was concerned, she let this shit happen by somehow allowing an unseelie into the human realm. But was this the reason she wanted her people to return to the Otherworld? Was she aware of the Society's rise and trying to stop it?

Colin smiled at me somewhat sadly. "You have so little faith."

I snorted, but William stepped in before I could shove my fist through Colin's face, even if I was too tied up to do it. I would have found a way…or used my boot in its place.

"It's time for games," their leader said. "Come and take your seats. Get comfortable. Maybe we'll even get some popcorn going."

One of the mages pushed me toward the seating, and I glared at him before complying. I honestly had no idea what I was going to do to get Thane and me out of here. Shifting into my bird form was always an option of course, but there was no way I could leave the reaper behind now. Those angels better hurry the fuck up.

I sat in the aqua leather seat the mage gestured to—front row luxury seating, of course. William followed me down but remained on his feet. He raised a hand toward the field again, held it dramatically like the pompous ass he had shown himself to be, then dropped it like he was slicing through the air.

The men who ushered Thane onto the field cut through the ropes binding the reaper, then removed his gag. As Thane rubbed at the raw skin around his wrists, visible even from this distance, the other two retreated back where they came from and shut the doors behind them. The reaper was alone on the field with a horde of undead.

Fuck.

William lingered next to me, his eyes fixed on his army. On some silent cue from their master, the entire contingent of Risen turned to face the reaper. Thane's eyes lifted to meet mine, some unknown emotion flashing across his features.

Little did these arrogant mages know, I could end all of this—all of *them*—by going nuclear. Only that wasn't an option until I knew Thane would be safe from my blast, and my blaze had a far-reaching effect. Bringing down the entire stadium was a real possibility, just not while he was inside.

"How is this even remotely a fair fight?" I asked, my lungs tightening as I finally recognized a deep sorrow in the reaper's gaze—and regret.

William looked down at me, considering my words like I had asked some profound question. "You're right. It's not fair. Let's make it more even." He caught the eye of one of his guards, then pointed at me. "Cuff her."

Well, that certainly wasn't what I meant. I tried to leap up to stop them, but I found myself frozen in place once again, my feet glued to the floor. Out of my periphery, one of the mages held a staff pointed at me, chanting.

The guard William had spoken to approached me with a metal cuff he secured around my ankle. A heavy, lethargic sensation filled my limbs, along with dread.

An anti-shifting device. No more easy escape option. This shit was going downhill real fast.

Pulling my stiffened shoulder forward, the guard reached behind me to slice through my zip tie with a knife, though my arms remained stuck where they were. He pushed me backward again, my movements still restricted by the mage with the staff.

"Take her to the field with her little sword. It will be more fun if you think you have a chance," William said, holding up a hand to stop Colin's protests. "This is not up for debate. Find another girl to take to your bed."

The guard who cuffed me lifted me into his arms like a baby. Each step down to the field made me bounce uncomfortably in his hold. I looked up at him, gauging whether I would be able to sweet talk my way out of this, but his eyes were glued to my bouncing breasts.

"Help me out of here and they're all yours," I said in a sultry voice. Nothing was beneath me right now. Besides, I'd kill him before he ever touched them.

He laughed at me and tilted his head back toward the suites. "Plenty of tits to go around up there. I'll just enjoy the view."

When we reached the field, he dropped me unceremoniously onto the ground, tossing Lisa near me. Gritting my teeth as my tailbone and spine screamed from the ill treatment, I tipped over onto my side, my limbs still frozen. The guard's feet shuffled away and the magic holding me in place withdrew. I pushed myself up to my feet, wincing as my spine spasmed.

Across the field, Thane met my gaze again, the sadness gone. His new expression was unreadable, but I did my best to smile despite the anger bubbling within me. That they threatened the very existence of everything I loved with the destruction this undead horde would bring on the world filled me with vengeful wrath. My arms and legs, even my lips, trembled with the barely restrained fury.

More than even that though, everything in my body, mind, and soul screamed at me to keep the reaper alive. That his life and mine were intertwined, connected in some way I couldn't describe. I clenched my fists as the certainty grew. If necessary, I would give my life to save his. I just didn't know why.

William's voice called out above the din of the undead, "Let's play ball!"

CHAPTER 25

Wednesday Before Dawn

With the fae's dumbass shout—he hadn't even gotten the right sport—the Risen seemed to regain control of their limbs. They wasted no time before staggering in my direction. I bent to draw Lisa from her sheath, snatched one of the hidden butterfly knives tucked inside my bun, and rushed forward to greet the dead.

After flicking open the knife's blade, I stabbed the closest decaying man through the temple. The dim light in his eyes snuffed out as he fell to the ground. A bone-chilling howl rose above the grumbling din—a lone dead wolf calling to a pack he would never join again. My heart ached for him, but now was not the time to stop and get sentimental.

I couldn't shift because of the damn cuff they put on me—and I knew it would be futile and stupid to try and remove it while the Risen were closing in—but that didn't mean I was helpless, despite what my confidence crisis earlier tried to make me believe. Because they had been milling about the field beforehand, the walking dead were spread out enough that I could slash and jab, duck and then plunge my blades into their skulls or sweep Lisa through their necks. I took them down one by one as I made my way toward the reaper.

A clawed hand gripped at my arm, and I sliced at the wrist until it came free from the body. I whirled and plunged my knife into the Risen's forehead. Down she went and the hand followed a moment later.

I lost count of how many I killed, but the blades' handles grew slippery as I fought, blood and bits of guts caking my arms and hands. The wave of bodies never ceased, their arms outstretched toward me, their teeth gnashing as they sensed fresh blood. Mindless grumbling and muttering turned into predatory growling and groaning whenever they spotted me.

As I took down another, a brief hole opened up and I tried to wipe my palms on my pants, only to spread the gore through even more gore. My clothes and skin were beyond disgusting. I gripped my blades tighter, hoping I could last even just a little longer.

Something slammed into me, knocking me to the ground. My butterfly knife skidded out of reach, but I still had Lisa. I held the beast's jaws away from my face with one forearm against its collarbone. I cringed when the fetid teeth got close to my nose, but I didn't let go.

Snarling, the wolf snapped for my face again before letting out a gurgling whine as my blade found its throat. I pushed up through the skull until the wolf stopped struggling. Even dead and emaciated, it was fucking heavy. I grunted as I heaved the beast to the side, letting its weight roll the rest of the way off me.

I leaped to my feet just in time to face another Risen. I didn't think I would be so relieved to face a human, but that werewolf had been much faster than the rest. My arms and legs burned with the exertion, but I had trained them well.

Something bumped into my shoulder, and I whirled around, only to come face-to-face with the reaper.

Thane.

My eyes met his and it felt like everything else fell away, that time stopped and it was just him and me, and a horde of Risen wasn't surrounding us. Even through the swelling from his beating, his eyes called to me like the ocean called to my soul, their blue the same hue as the deep waters off the coast. Impossible as it seemed, my pulse raced even faster in his presence, my heart thudding against my ribs.

"Veronica Neill, what in the seven hells are you doing here?" he asked, lifting a hand to brush an errant and bloody strand of hair away from my face. I leaned into his touch like a lovesick puppy.

When I opened my mouth to answer, I realized the world had actually fallen silent. I glanced around me. Time had stopped for everything except him and me. Risen held their arms out toward us, a few fingers about to brush against me but held in a moment of time.

"What's happening?" I asked. Reapers having the ability to stop time was news to me.

"It won't last long," he said, drawing my attention back to his face, the angles made almost more beautiful by the shading of the bruises. "But I needed to see you first."

"Why?" The word barely came out in a soft breath.

"To do this." He lifted his hands to my face, pulling me in closer and placing his lips against mine.

An inferno engulfed me, sparks igniting from my head down to my toes. I dropped my blade and wrapped my arms around his neck, pressing against his chest, wanting to feel the hardness of his muscles, the realness of who he was.

Our tongues met and explored each other, our kiss becoming hungrier and deeper the longer we stayed connected. He tasted of salt and heat and metal, the ocean breeze warmed by the rays of the sun. He tasted like home, and I wanted to taste all of him and him all of me. I wrapped my fingers in his hair and gripped tight, as if I could hold him even closer.

He groaned against my lips before pulling away, leaving me breathless and off balance. I stared at him, panting.

"Better than I expected for a last kiss," he said with his familiar smirk.

I took a deep breath and rolled my eyes. "We're not going to die."

"No?" His face grew strained for a moment. "I can only hold this for another minute at best."

"You know your scythe would have done so much more damage than your bare hands," I said, avoiding looking at the state of his clothes after I had pressed myself against him. They were already in a tattered, bloody state before I arrived, but now…

His mouth parted in surprise, and he laughed. "Even if I wasn't relieved of my blade and ability to teleport myself out of here, there are too many for us to take by ourselves, no matter how good a fighter you think you are."

I waved my hand dismissively and bent to pick up my sword. When I had pressed myself against him, I had also felt my family's talisman that I gave him before facing Xavier. He still wore it, a fact that made my insides quiver and my face want to grin like an idiot.

But even better, I knew he would live.

"You don't know everything about me, reaper." I let a devious smile curl my lips.

His returning smirk made the butterflies in my stomach spin up in a new dance. "I'd like to know more."

"You ready for the show of your life?"

He raised an eyebrow. "Are you about to do a strip tease or something?"

The horde moved a fraction of an inch as his concentration slipped, and I laughed.

"Maybe someday." I winked at him. We would live, if only because I needed to finish what we started here with that kiss.

When I turned to face the mages in the suites, I found William's frozen face and smiled. "You can unstop time now."

CHAPTER 26

Wednesday Before Dawn

Nine years had come and gone in the blink of an eye, yet somehow also lasted an eternity. Nine years since I last did what I was about to attempt, and back then it was to say goodbye to two of the most important people in my life.

No living human being would have been alive the last time a phoenix resurrected outside the returning-to-the-sun ceremony. Those present were about to get the show of their lives, and also their last if the gods were watching and waiting—everyone except Thane. I smiled.

Before half-rotten hands could grab either of us again as the reaper released his hold on time, I called upon the living fire that writhed inside me. The phoenix magic knew what I intended to do, and it was hungry to answer my call. My entire body burst into flames, a blaze that reached out and licked those close enough to touch. The fire spread quickly thanks to the dry skin and tattered clothes of the Risen.

But that was just the start.

The inferno of my body grew, engulfing my entire being down to my soul. I called out to Ognebog, invoking his flames to grow within me as the horde continued to close in, not reacting in panic to the fire. They had no concept of fear and pain. Some fell as their bodies burned, becoming molten obstacles for those pressing in behind, and flurries of ash danced into the air. The chaos of it all worked in my favor.

I raised my arms to the sky, calling on Dazhbog's early morning rays to bring me forth once again. My body lifted off the ground as if raised by the gods themselves, decaying hands still reaching toward me through the flames. As I rose above their heads, I found William's ice-blue gaze through the fire and smoke. His lips were pressed tight in a thin line but his eyes were calculating and filled with rapturous desire as he recognized what I was at last.

Too late.

I rose above the field toward the predawn sky, knowing Thane was doing his best to fend off the Risen ready to swallow him whole. I only had a finite amount of time until they succeeded. The fire engulfing my very essence burned brighter, a hungry flame devouring the oxygen around us as it grew.

Calling on all the phoenix gods as the power grew to bursting within me, I flipped in the air and hurled myself toward the ground, a fireball streaking down from the sky. Just before I connected with the earth, Thane went down, overtaken at last.

I hit the grass and exploded like a bomb.

The fire that had enveloped me blazed out around me, incinerating everything it touched, smoke and ash crashing over and engulfing the army of Risen in inky darkness. The boom of the explosion rocked the stadium and sent signs and seats crashing, collapsing several of the suites' roofs.

Then my world went black as night and blissfully silent.

I wasn't alone, though. Mokosh, the ancient mother goddess of my people, wrapped me in her warm embrace like a womb. I floated weightless and formless in time and space, warmth filling my entire being, down to my soul. I wanted to stay there forever, feeling loved and free of pain or fear or worry for the rest of my life.

Except I had a job to do, a purpose to see to the end. These motherfuckers would pay.

My world spun and lightning shot through my being, striking to my core. There was a reason my kind reserved rebirths for scenarios of life or death. I was incorporeal but a scream of agony tore through my mind as bolts continued to strike, rebuilding my body from the sun's fire that created us. As each new bone grew from my core, muscles and tendons stretched to fit, securing it all together. It was excruciating, burning hotter than the sun and colder than the iciest tundra all at once.

Rebuilding only took a matter of seconds, but in my mind, the pain lasted a lifetime.

When I opened my eyes again, I lay on my side on the football field, the ground scratchy beneath my bare skin. The lacerations that had criss-crossed my arms were replaced by new, fresh skin, and gone was the golden tan I had worked so hard to get. That last fact was the least of my worries right now, but damn, it had taken years to perfect.

Beneath a haze of grey and white, the grass that should have been all around me was gone. Charred earth, soot, and bones replaced the green, extending to the edges of the field. Most of the Risen were gone; only a few corpses remained near the far edges of the field, missing legs or even whole torsos.

I glanced up toward the suites where the mages had been, but no faces looked back. Blood and guts splattered across the seats and walls of the suites. With any luck, my explosion had taken out some of the mages, too. Maybe even William, though I doubted I was that lucky.

I struggled to my feet, my legs feeling a bit like I imagined a just-born foal would feel, wobbly and weak. A hand supported me beneath my elbow, and I whipped around, stumbling slightly, to face Thane.

The reaper stared at me as he released my elbow. I was naked, but it wasn't my body he was staring at. It was just me.

"What in God's name are you?" he asked, something like fear and awe vying for space in his tone.

I looked him straight in the eye. "The last phoenix."

He pulled off the tatters of his shirt and held it out to me, his eyes and expression still trying to figure out what to make of me. My gaze drifted to his abs and the deep slashes there, a product of his torture, and I had the sudden urge to lick his wounds. It might have sounded gross, but being a shifter, I knew it to be an instinctual response that animals and humans alike shared. I wanted to heal him, to make him feel better.

My finger grazed his as I took the shirt, sparks practically igniting between us again to race through my arm and straight down my wobbling legs. Everything tingled as I slipped the shirt over my head and looked down with a chuckle. The strips of fabric didn't cover much, but it would be a small start. A very small start. At least it came down to my thighs.

"How am I still standing?" he asked, looking at the devastated field around us with disbelief. Teeth marks lined his arms and shoulders, some gouged down to the bone.

I tapped the talisman against his bare chest, careful not to touch his very-tempting skin for fear I would do so much more. The charm's metal displayed an image of phoenix wings spread before the sun. To the uneducated, which was most people, it just looked like a bird of prey. "This protects you against phoenix fire. I'm glad you decided to keep it on."

He looked down at the necklace, shock written across his bruised face.

"V!" Kit's voice called out across the field. She stood at the edge of the wall separating the field from the first row of seating. No angels in sight.

After I grabbed Lisa—the blade had been imbued with magic to protect it from the heat of a phoenix inferno—Thane and I ran over to the wall which was also covered in blood, scorch marks, and pieces of charred skin. The reaper helped me up and over thanks to my shaking legs, and I didn't even care what kind of view that move gave him.

He pulled himself up and landed on light feet next to me.

"Since we had planned on this being a sneak in, sneak out mission, I hadn't thought to bring a change of clothes," Kit said, eyeing my tattered shirt and Thane's bare chest.

"Me either. Guess I'll be streaking through Miami." I smiled before I remembered she was supposed to bring backup. "Where's Adam?"

"Like I would actually leave you here," she said with a shake of her head. "Just like you wouldn't leave him behind."

Thane opened his mouth to say something, but Kit started poking and prodding at him. Checking the extent of his injuries, I assumed. He hissed and winced as she found an especially tender spot on his ribs. When he found his voice again, he said, "They used poison to counteract my healing ability. We need to call Adam."

"We have to get out first. There's no cell signal here." Kit knelt down and dug around in her bag of supplies. "They must have done something to jam it."

After pulling out a bottle and a few bandages, she applied the same foul-smelling paste she had used on me after an encounter with a manticore left a hole in my shoulder. She wrapped up his chest and a few other oozing wounds. He grimaced at the vomit-like scent but didn't say anything. Nicer reaction than I'd had.

His deep ocean-colored eyes never left mine, almost like staring at me grounded him somehow. I still hadn't had the right opportunity to ask him if he felt any of the things I did when we touched, primarily the intense heat with or without a kiss. At least now I knew he was into me and not just trying to get my help on a case. A fact which had me biting my lip and picking at one of the loose threads on the end of the shirt.

Now was most certainly not the right time to ask about it all, but my cheeks grew warm under his gaze, knowing we would have another chance. Provided we escaped.

"The mages are regrouping. We gotta move," Kit said after putting her supplies away. She withdrew a throwing knife from her bag and handed it to me. It was like she knew I would feel naked without one, disregarding the fact that I was still basically naked in Thane's tattered shirt.

My legs had grown sturdier as Kit administered to Thane's wounds, so I had no issues with wobbling legs as I followed her toward the doors leading into the main hallways. But before I went through, I stopped to glance back at the VIP suites. I caught a glimpse of William barking orders at the others around him, including Colin. Anger rose within me hard and fast as I narrowed my eyes at the man who had betrayed me. The angrier I got, the steadier my legs grew.

We would meet again.

The hallway was silent and empty, but paranoia kept the hairs on the back of my neck from lying flat. Mages or mercenaries would be coming before long, some of them fae, which would make escaping much more difficult.

We moved quickly down the hall, the stench of rotting flesh replaced with the thickness of smoke. Soot and ash covered the floor and walls, still settling like grey and black snowflakes as we headed toward the closest exit. We had studied the blueprints, but there were also signs pointing the way. Our footsteps barely echoed against the wide-open area and cement floors.

The exit came into view, as did three guards stationed there, surveying the area outside the stadium. They grew still as a garbled voice came through on their radios, then they turned around, now facing the hallway, their eyes roving. A shout rang out as one of them spotted us.

My magic would take some time to replenish after the resurrection, but that didn't mean I couldn't fight. Without hesitation, I ran toward them, my bare feet slapping against the cement. I threw my knife at the closest one as I ran, and the blade embedded in his throat, straight through his Adam's apple.

He dropped his gun as he raised his hands, trying to block the blood gushing out. His gasping gurgles filled the air as I slid on the ground like I was sliding across home base. In any other scenario, a move like that while pantsless would be painful, but today the cement was covered in a layer of slick soot.

I leaped to my feet and spun in a circle with Lisa, decapitating one who stared in shock at his dying peer. Probably a mage who wasn't used to seeing his friends die. Now he wouldn't have to again. The last man got a thrust through his chest, my blade coming out his back. I twisted the hilt to ensure his death and pulled Lisa back out as he slumped to the ground.

I wasn't a murderer, but this is what I had been trained to do and my purpose in life: defend the ones I loved. I wouldn't focus too much on the fact that meant the goddamn reaper had wormed a place into my heart before all of this and that kiss on the field went and solidified it.

With Kit and Thane reaching my side, we ran out into the open air, the encroaching dawn lighting our way.

CHAPTER 27

Wednesday Pre-Dawn

As soon as we reached the safety of Kit's motorcycle, she pulled out her cell phone to call Adam. While she spoke quietly to the archangel, I turned to Thane. "Let's regroup at the DEA."

He needed to check in and let his boss and the others know what was happening with the fae and the Society, and Kit and I needed a safe place to rest and recover. My penthouse was probably equally as safe, but Kit would have to drive Thane, and I didn't want to let either of them out of my sight just yet.

However, I wouldn't be able to get anywhere with this goddamn anti-shifting cuff still attached. Of course it just *had* to stick with me through a fucking resurrection.

When Kit tucked her phone away, I asked, "Do you have a backup lockpick?"

"I have backups for my backups." She dug through her bag and handed me the lockpick set, and I got to work on the cuff at my feet. After my inferno didn't do the trick, I knew the magic imbued in the metal kept me from being able to melt the damn thing off.

"I can help with that," Thane said, crouching down next to me.

The angle was a little tricky, but I had picked harder locks. I didn't feel the need to tell him that, though, as I handed the pick and wrench over to him. He took my ankle in one hand to pull it closer to him, running his thumb over my skin. The shock of his touch raced up my leg to pool in my core, instantly warming every inch of me.

When the lock clicked open, he carefully pulled off the cuff and gave it and the set back to Kit. Despite the raw skin around his wrists, he massaged my ankle like I had suffered the same. Far from it, and definitely not now that he was touching me.

Every move he made against my skin sent tingles up my leg to my most sensitive places, fire surging through every inch, my body shaking with anticipation and need. As his hands moved up my calves, he watched my face, my breath coming out in small gasps. His lips raised in the smallest of smirks, as if he knew exactly what he was doing to me. A blaze raged inside me, desperate to be released.

"You ready?" Kit asked, too busy digging through her bag for her keys to realize she had basically ruined my moment.

Thane set my foot down and stood, then reached a hand

toward me. I took a deep, shuddering breath, glad for the interruption before I did something crazy like take the reaper for a ride right in front of my best friend, before accepting his hand and getting to my feet.

With a final glance at Thane, whose bandaged and shirtless chest kept my desire and womanly needs alive and well, I shifted into my bird form and took to the skies. Kit started up the bike, and the reaper climbed on behind her. The bike's engine roared as she took off down the street, and I followed above them, my gaze scouring the roads ahead.

Traffic hadn't gotten terrible yet due to the hour of the day, the sun not yet peeking over the horizon. Our trip downtown to the government quarter was relatively short, but still provided enough time to cool down the volcanic eruption threatening to boil over inside of me. I swooped under the ceiling of the garage as they pulled in and parked, no longer feeling like I would immediately jump the reaper for a quickie.

After landing beside the bike, I shifted back into my human form, trying unsuccessfully to cover more of my bits with the tattered shirt. I was sure I would offend or distract a newer reaper or two, but the angels had no issue with nudity. Humanity came that way, after all.

As we approached the door leading into the offices, it burst open and Jessa rushed out, her hands shooing us away.

"You need to go," she said, coming right up to me and spinning me around, back toward the street.

"What? Why?" I asked, though I didn't resist. Her tone sent shivers down my spine, and I turned my head to glance at her lightly freckled face.

"Everyone knows you're a phoenix," she said, looking me in the eye. Fear shone through.

"How?"

"Your friend Colin arrived a few minutes ago," she explained. "He's been working secretly with Adam as a double agent, infiltrating the Society of the Dead."

My mouth hung open stupidly. That was completely unexpected and sent my thoughts into a whirlwind. I still hated him. Maybe. Did I? I didn't know just yet.

"He announced the reality of who you are in front of a handful of reapers," she continued with a sigh, "not realizing that Adam already knew and wanted it kept a secret."

"How does a handful become everyone?" Thane asked, coming in closer.

"The necromancers' leader announced it on the Community forums, putting a hefty bounty on Veronica's head before Adam could shut it down." Jessa paused for a moment. "He's not the most pleasant archangel to be around right now."

"Wouldn't the agency still be the safest place for her?" Thane asked, glancing between me and the angel. I was glad he could think through this whole situation because my thoughts were still a jumbled mess.

"Adam wants her here, and I trust him, but..." she trailed off, biting her lip as she glanced around.

"What is it?" Kit asked.

"My instinct is telling me it's not safe for her here," Jessa said, meeting my gaze. "I can only assume His Holiness is sending me a message."

"He doesn't talk to you directly?" I couldn't stop the snarky tone that came with the question, so I gave her an apologetic grimace instead.

"That would make things far simpler, but no," Jessa said with an understanding smile. "Faith is a requirement of the job. Now, go to your safe house."

"You know about it?" Both my eyebrows rose. I really shouldn't have been surprised, but I honestly thought I had been more than careful.

"Only me." She winked. "I made sure of that."

"Okay, so I go back to my place, and then what?"

"Then you wait."

"For what?"

The angel sighed and put her hands on her hips. "Veronica Neill, you are far too much trouble for being the last of your kind. You wait until I tell you otherwise, that's what."

I couldn't hold back a sheepish grin. She was completely right, after all.

I had every intention of obeying Jessa and staying put in my penthouse, but after a shower, change of clothes, hearty breakfast, and an hour spent staring out at the ocean on my terrace chaise, I was beyond done doing nothing. Yeah, it would suck if I went and got myself killed and the phoenix species became truly extinct like everyone believed up until today. But it was also incredibly difficult to really kill me, and I was willing to bet most people didn't know how.

I grabbed my phone off the side table and called Tabitha.

"Veronica?" her tone was incredulous. "Is it true?"

"Depends on what you heard," I said. "But I need you to meet me at Luka's house right away." She paused, so I jumped in again before she could say no, "It's a matter of life and death."

"I'll be there as soon as I can," she sighed. "But I—"

I hung up without another word, hoping it would add to the mystery of my cryptic call. After shifting into my bird form, I dove off my terrace, swooped over the ocean once, then swung back up and toward the alpha werewolf's house on the outskirts of the city.

Once again, the block on stilts seemed deserted from up above, but I knew better. I landed on the dirt and gravel in front of his house and let out a screech that shook the windows. Three grey and brown wolves bounded toward me from the surrounding trees, their lips curled up into vicious snarls. I shifted back into my human form and stared them down.

All three came to a halt and circled me, saliva dripping from their mouths. They knew I was a phoenix now, but they didn't know exactly what that meant as a threat.

The front door opened, and Luka stepped out in jeans and a white t-shirt that contrasted beautifully against his russet skin, anger giving way to surprise on his face. Beneath his wavy black hair, amber eyes regarded me for a moment before he came down the steps to face me directly, albeit a foot taller and much wider than me.

"I didn't expect to see you again," he said with his thick Spanish accent.

"Yeah, well, I'm here to see our deal through."

Luka sighed. "It's not a deal, Ms. Neill."

A beat-up blue sedan pulled up the long gravel drive and parked. Tabitha stepped out, her honey-hued eyes moving between me and Luka.

"You said it was a matter of life and death," she said, not moving out from behind the open car door. She had worn her long, dark-brown hair in a thick braid, and she picked at the end as she glanced between us.

"It is." I pointed at Luka. "He's threatening to kill me if you don't return to the pack."

Her eyes widened as she looked at her alpha. "It wasn't her fault. I asked her to steal the ring."

Before he could reprimand her, I held up a hand. "I take full responsibility for my actions. But Luka, please tell Tabitha how you feel about her. How you *really* feel."

He sighed and rubbed his neck. When he dropped his hand again, he looked her straight in the eye. "My love for you endures. Nothing will change that."

And now for the super tense moment. I bit my lip. An alpha wolf declaring his love for his desired mate was huge. If she turned him down, he would be shamed in front of his pack. He would have one of two choices: kill her to reassert his dominance or leave the pack. No one ever said werewolves were known for their cuddly nature.

Good thing I knew she still felt the same way about him. Maybe I was better at reading people than I gave myself credit for. Did I smell a new career as a couples' mediator or as a Community matchmaker?

She didn't drop his gaze, but tears wet her cheeks. "You know I love you, too, but I can't do this. Not after what happened. I need to protect my son."

"Come home, and the ring is yours," Luka said.

Tabitha hesitated.

"Tell her the truth about her father, Luka," I said before she had the chance to run away again.

He glanced sharply at me, eyebrows furrowing. "How do you know?"

I shrugged. "I'm just that good." Also, I had an amazing best friend who could hack into the DEA files regarding this issue, but I liked the mystery of it all better. It was good for business.

Luka faced Tabitha once again. "Your father went into a frenzy."

Tabitha placed a hand over her mouth and closed her eyes, a sob shaking her shoulders.

The term 'going into a frenzy' meant roughly the same to the wolves as it did anyone else—he went crazy. It wasn't common with wolves, more so with regular shifters like myself, but there was no cure. Once the mania set in, the berserker needed to be put down. With an alpha wolf becoming frenzied, thought to be a result of genetics, the entire pack would have been shamed before the other clans as a sign of their pack's weakness.

What Luka did was wise and merciful to all his wolves, and especially to Tabitha and her son. As the frenzied wolf's blood relatives, he would have had to banish them to try to save face with the other clans if anyone found out about her father.

The alpha walked over to Tabitha and took her in his arms, stroking her hair as she cried. Our eyes met over the top of her head and he gave me a quick nod. Their story might not have a perfect happy ending, but they would still be happy. And damn, their cubs would be absolutely adorable.

My work here was done.

CHAPTER 28

Wednesday Afternoon

I held up my hands in surrender. "I had to, I swear. The alpha wolf would have killed me next."

Jessa pinched the bridge of her freckled nose. She, Thane, and Kit had all been waiting for me in my living room when I returned to my penthouse, yet she was the only one who had expected me to actually listen to her command to stay put. Thane had a smirk on his face from his sprawled-out place on one of the living room chairs, and Kit ignored us all from behind her laptop screen at the dining room table.

"Do I even want to know why Luka Navarro was going to kill you?" the angel asked.

"Probably not."

"Okay, then let's move on to what's going to happen from here." She pointed at my L-shaped couch and I obeyed this time. Sitting felt really good after the night I had. She continued, "I spoke with Adam and he agrees that it's not safe for you here anymore."

"Here meaning my penthouse?"

"Miami." She shook her head when I opened my mouth to protest. "Not up for debate. You will be moving to… Where again?" Jessa turned her questioning gaze on Kit.

"Tucson," my ex-best friend-turned-traitor replied.

"Where the fuck is that?" I asked.

"Arizona."

"You want me to leave paradise for the fucking desert?" I leaned back into the couch pillow and crossed my arms. "Not gonna happen."

Jessa let out a sound of frustration, somewhere between a sigh and a groan. "It's not up for debate, Veronica. You're going. Adam made a promise to protect you, and now you've gone and gotten yourself a giant target on your back."

I frowned. "Who did he promise?"

Her blue-green eyes softened. "Your parents."

My jaw dropped open. "And you've been keeping this from me?"

"You seem to forget that I work for the archangel," Jessa said, putting her hands on her hips. "Being your friend comes second."

Ouch. I didn't blame her, of course, but Adam wasn't here to answer my questions. To answer for his deception.

Before I could ask anything else, she headed for my bedroom and called out over her shoulder, "Where do you keep your suitcases?"

I stared at her wings until she disappeared into the room, my lips pressed firmly together.

"I thought your kind liked the heat," Thane said, his grin speaking volumes about how much he enjoyed my frustration.

I gave him my best glare. "The desert is a dry heat."

He stood from his chair and approached the couch, his deep blue eyes lightening to a sapphire as he stared me down. He sat beside me, his warmth radiating into me. "You need to go."

"Why?" Stubborn might not have been my finest trait, but it was one of the oldest. I would be damned if I was going to let it go anytime soon.

He brushed my hair back from my face and tucked it behind my ear, the light yet still fiery touch of his fingers sending shivers down my back. "Because it's not safe here, and we need you to be safe."

I rolled my eyes. "Well, *we* can mind our own business and let me make my own decisions about my life."

The back of his hand stroked my jaw, leaving a scorching trail until he gripped my chin. He held it firmly as he leaned in, his lips so close I could feel each warm breath he exhaled. Spicy cardamom mixed with the sweetness of bergamot. "*I* need you to be safe."

"Why?" I whispered, my breath coming out shallow.

His lips, soft and sensual, pressed against mine, lightly at first, as if testing it out, then with more urgency. I responded hungrily, my mouth parting and my tongue flicking out to trace his lips. His hand slid behind my neck, holding me to him, the burn of his grip sending shockwaves through my body. I wanted to climb into his lap, wrap my arms around his neck, and feel his arousal pressed against me.

But we weren't alone. The clicking of Kit's keyboard grew incessantly louder until it was impossible to ignore. I broke the kiss, pulled back against his hand, and stared into his eyes. We were both breathless, his face flushed with a matching desire and need.

"What are you doing to me?" he asked quietly, pressing his forehead to mine.

I wasn't quite sure if that was him admitting he felt the same intense heat and the need to feel more as I did, or a simple admission that this wasn't such a great idea—him being an infertile reaper and me being the last of my kind and needing to procreate someday and all. The actual phoenix mating ritual was blessed by the gods and used magic that wouldn't last outside my body in a petri dish. I let out a deep sigh.

Regardless, I needed to leave Miami. Not for my safety, but the safety of my kind. I couldn't let anything more happen with the beautiful reaper, not even a one-night stand. Because I knew deep down, it would never end with a one-night stand.

If we took it any further, I would never be able to let him go.

"Repeat them back to me again," Kit said as she walked me into Miami International Airport, a move I told her was absolutely ridiculous. I was more than capable of getting myself safely onto an airplane.

"I know the rules. I've repeated them three times now," I said with a huff, blowing my newly dark brown hair out of my face. Dyeing my way-too-recognizable white-blonde locks was one of several moves we made to hide my identity from bounty hunters. I eyed the different counters until I found my airline to check my two bags.

"Then you won't have a problem doing it again."

I sighed and got in line to hand over my bags. "This is silly, you know."

Kit just waited.

"Fine. No walking alone at night, no logging into Community forums or websites, only use cash, no phone calls home."

"And?" Kit raised an eyebrow at me.

I gave her my best glare, but she didn't back down. "No shifting unless my life is on the line."

She nodded, satisfied, and moved one of my bags forward in the line. Almost there.

"Technically, my life is on the line just being alive."

Kit turned to give me a frosty look. "Don't you dare try to create a loophole. You know exactly what it means."

"Okay, *Jessa*." I had no intention of disobeying, but then the road to hell was paved with good intentions. Time would tell if I had finally learned to play by the rules.

Rolling her eyes, she lifted my bag onto the scale as if it weighed next to nothing. 49 pounds. I lifted the other one with a bit more of a struggle. 47.5 pounds. Damn, she was strong. Maybe I would work on my strength while I was banished. Exiled, even.

I finished up with the person at the counter, then walked with Kit toward security. She reached over and took my hand, holding it firmly like she was afraid to let me go.

"I would say I'll call you when I land, but…" I gave her a small smile as I got in line.

She followed along the outside of the rope. "Don't do anything stupid, V. Please. For me."

I met her pleading eyes, feeling like someone was squeezing my lungs. Kit was scared.

"I promise," I said and raised both hands to show I wasn't crossing any fingers. I blew her a kiss when I reached the guy checking IDs and tickets. After I finished unloading all my things onto the conveyor belt, I glanced back at Kit, but she was gone.

It had been years since my heart felt this heavy. I was leaving my whole life behind me because some maniacal fae mage named Bill the Necromancer couldn't listen to his superiors. I was all about revolutions when things actually needed them, but I couldn't agree that his lot in life as one of the immortal fae necessitated a revolution, especially using an army of the undead to make it happen.

I stepped through the metal detector when it was my turn, then gathered my personal things again and headed for the gate. I would be taking a flight to Dallas, then renting a car with a fake name and fake ID to drive the rest of the way to Tucson. From everything I had seen on the map, the drive would be boring as fuck.

As I settled into an empty seat to wait for boarding, I stared out the window and watched the activities on the tarmac. What I should have done was move to a private, super remote island, with one very sexy grim reaper by my side. Only that last part wasn't even remotely a possibility, which meant I had accepted exile to the desert. We had said our goodbyes and that was that. If only my heart would stop hurting every time I thought of him.

I could have avoided the airplane and rental car altogether and flown myself in bird form, except the agency had caught wind of bounty hunters looking to the skies with catapults and nets at the ready. It was far safer to stay hidden as a human for now, not to mention it would have been difficult to take much with me. And I still would have had to stop for rest and food.

I caught my eyes in the window reflection, brown contacts matching the brown of my hair. Add in the loss of my tan, and I was a brand-new person.

Nah. Traveling this way was the safest bet, and I would be settling into my new life in just a few days.

I sighed. This sucked.

CHAPTER 29

Tuesday Morning

If I thought Miami was hot, Tucson was turning out to be even hotter, and it was only June. The locals had been completely right when they warned me about the dry heat. Sticking one's head in an oven would probably feel better to most people. Good thing I didn't mind it one bit.

I continued to stock the shelves of Antigone Books, a Tucson icon since the '70s. I had debated for a while whether or not to get a job at a coffee shop, but I decided that might be too obvious for anyone who came looking for me. Books weren't exactly my thing, but I enjoyed a good contemporary romcom here and there when I could get my dyslexia to stop messing with the words. Audiobooks were a godsend.

The popular 4th Avenue shop was right up my alley, opened by three women and named for a mythological character who stood her ground against male authority figures. Yep, definitely a place I could call my new home. Not that I lived in the shop. My place was walking distance, though, several stories up in one of the newer downtown apartments. I needed to have a little bit of the big-city feel, after all.

I placed another stack of books on a shelf and pushed the cart wielding boxes full of dead trees toward the next aisle. Tucson was a beautiful, eclectic town with amazing mountains I hadn't realized surrounded the entire area. But it wasn't home. The scents were weird, the animals even weirder, and the people were a strange mix of cowboys, *chicanos*, and college kids. Like Miami, the snowbirds were making their summer migration north into cooler temperatures.

Snowbirds meaning old people, of course.

At least the food was good. Cuban food was still better, in my not-so-humble opinion, but the more I explored the city over the past week with the primary goal of eating my way through it, the more I enjoyed my stay.

But hot damn, I was *bored*. For the last three years, my life had been one of adventure and excitement and danger. It was sexy and thrilling. Now, I was stacking books on shelves, ringing up customers, and trying to get the lay of the land in a city I wasn't super excited to be in. Nor the reason for it all. I wasn't even allowed to spread my wings and fly, a rule that made me feel caged.

I was stuck here while my best friend and pseudo-partner at the agency were off looking for where the necromancers' Society of the Dead had holed up after we outed their stadium hideout. My friends were off having the adventure of a lifetime, and even Luka's wolf pack had joined in on the hunt. I liked to think I had a hand in helping them become better allies to the agency.

With a quiet grumble, I placed another book on the shelf.

At least Kit wouldn't make any moves on Thane. The mere thought of him sent shivers of heat through my body, and I let out a deep sigh.

"Everything okay, Maddie?" Ashley's voice called out across the shelf.

"Yeah, sorry, I was just thinking about a book I have at home that I, uh, couldn't put down," I said, stumbling through an answer that was foreign to me.

I had assumed the name Madison Fox because it sounded glamorous while also constantly reminding me of my brother, my sword Lisa, and the true reason for being here. If I died, Mad's death would never be avenged.

Ashley laughed. "I know that feeling. What book?"

I stared at the cookbook in my hand, caught. "Uh, The Reaper's Kiss."

Fuck.

"Never heard of it," she said.

"Yeah, it's, uh, more of the supernatural romance stuff."

"You should talk to my friend Gary about it…" her voice rambled on about the books Gary enjoyed reading while my thoughts drifted back to the reaper once again.

Someday, I would get to return to Miami. Someday, I would figure out what the hell was going on between me and Thane. I closed my eyes and let the accompanying heat wash over me, tingling through my limbs and accumulating between my legs.

Someday better come soon.

I love to get to know my readers. You can reach me on Facebook, Instagram, or Twitter **@stephaniemirro**. Sign up for my mailing list to get new release information, special deals, giveaways, become a part of my ARC team, and more. I look forward to hearing from you!

www.stephaniemirro.com

Veronica's story continues in…

WINGS
OF
WINTER

THE LAST PHOENIX: BOOK THREE

GLOSSARY

Adam Larue – Archangel of Miami

Albert Renauldo, Dr. – human plastic surgeon; owns Star Island mansion

Anthony "Tony" – piano shop owner; friend of Veronica

Broderick Ó Faoláin – fae duke; *deceased*

Colin Ó Broin

Death Enforcement Agency – also known as the DEA; agency of the human world that keeps the Community safe

Drystan Neill – father of Veronica; *deceased*

El Sombra Mercado – also known as the Shadow Market

Enrique Alvarez – human street musician

Frank Turner – human mage; ex-necromancer

Giovanni "Joe" Facchini – fae regular of The Morning

Grind; friend of Veronica

Isaac Davidson – human manager of The Morning Grind; boss of Veronica

Jackson Reed – realm walker; in prison

Jessa – healing angel

Katherine "Kit" Parker – natural born witch; best friend of Veronica

Luciana Pérez – natural born witch; owner of The Witch's Brew shop in *el Sombra Mercado*

Luka Navarro – alpha of the Miami werewolf pack

Maddox "Mad" Neill – brother of Veronica; *deceased*

Manuel – owner of food truck in *el Sombra Mercado*

Nathan – fighting angel

Officer Harris – receptionist at prison; species unknown but most likely a troll

Owen Cooper, Dr. – head mortician and grim reaper at the DEA

Rhiannon Neill – mother of Veronica; *deceased*

Rogelio Diaz – natural born warlock; deep in his cup somewhere

Sophia Clark – grim reaper agent of the DEA

Tabitha Delgado – werewolf

Thane Munro – grim reaper agent of the DEA

The Morning Grind – a DC-based coffee shop in Miami; Veronica's day job

Veronica "V" Neill – the last phoenix

William Caomhánach – Winter Court fae and unseelie

Xavier Garcia – Master Vampire of Miami

ACKNOWLEDGEMENTS

To my entire family, who continue to show their never-ending love and support, *thank you.*

To my editor, Renee Dugan, my proofreader, Renee Regent; and my beta readers, Marty, Leilani, Tom, Kimmie, Jessica, Michelle, Alisha, Rachel, Devon, Lauren, Erica, Vicki, and Erin, *thank you.*

To Claire Holt of Luminescence Covers, who brought Veronica to life with this stunning cover, *thank you.*

To all my family and friends, who showed their support in so many ways—asking how writing was going, becoming Patrons on Patreon, and following me on all things social media—*thank you.*

To you, my dear reader, for picking up this book and making it through to the end, *thank you.*

I'm going to go cry now.

ABOUT THE AUTHOR

Stephanie Mirro's lifetime love of ancient mythology led to her majoring in the Classics in college, which wasn't quite as much fun as writing her own mythology stories as she did growing up. But that education, combined with an overactive imagination, being an active fantasy reader, and having a vampire obsession, resulted in the *Immortal Relics* series.

Born and raised in Southern Arizona, Stephanie now resides in Northern Virginia with her husband, two kids, and two furbabies. This thing called "seasons" is still magical.

www.ingramcontent.com/pod-product-compliance
Lightning Source LLC
Chambersburg PA
CBHW021312190726
48288CB00003B/807